# JIMMY'S CURSE

LIZARDVILLE GHOST STORIES BOOK 2

# STEVE ALTIER

4 Horsemen Publications, Inc.
1497 Main St. Suite 169
Dunedin, FL 34698
4horsemenpublications.com
info@4horsemenpublications.com

Cover & Typesetting by Autumn Skye
Edited by Gayle Staggemeyer



*Library of Congress Control Number: 2023936331*

*Paperback ISBN-13: 979-8-8232-0164-3*
*Hardcover ISBN-13: 979-8-8232-0166-7*
*Audiobook ISBN-13: 979-8-8232-0163-6*
*Ebook ISBN-13: 979-8-8232-0165-0*

# DEDICATION

To Jessica Altier

Thank you for your help and support.

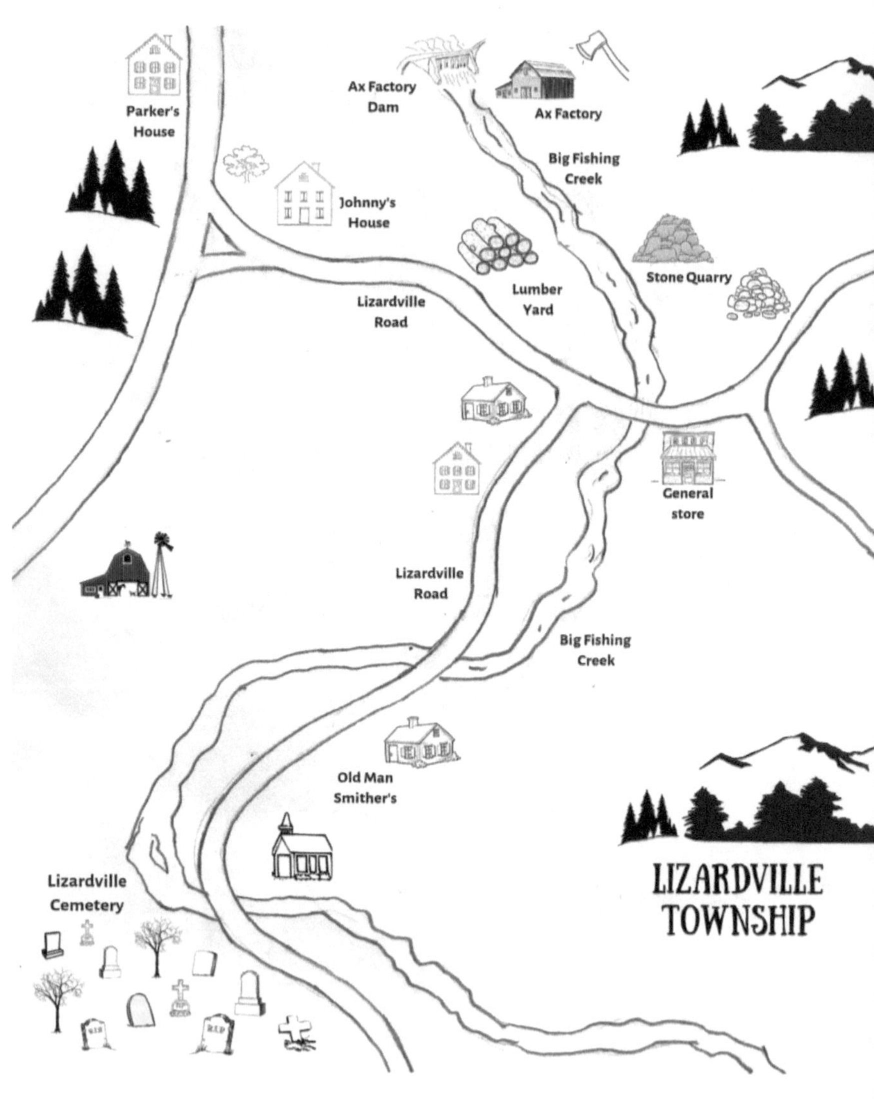

Parker's House
Ax Factory Dam
Ax Factory
Big Fishing Creek
Johnny's House
Lumber Yard
Stone Quarry
Lizardville Road
General store
Lizardville Road
Big Fishing Creek
Old Man Smither's
Lizardville Cemetery
R.I.P
R.I.P
LIZARDVILLE TOWNSHIP

# TABLE OF CONTENTS

# ONE

The storm raged on with a brilliant flash of light and a loud crack of thunder. Zack and Daniel sat quietly in the family room, watching the candle flicker. Sara and I prepared sandwiches in the kitchen, which was all we could muster since the electricity was out, and her time was short. Sara's smile could brighten any room, even on the dreariest days like today. It wouldn't be long before the boys' mother would have to return to the hospital.

Sara and I entered the room carrying drinks and a tray of sandwiches. The boys smiled. I'm sure they were hungry since I had overlooked fixing something for them to eat earlier. I'd lost track of time while telling them about my childhood. Each of the boys grabbed a sandwich and proceeded to wolf it down.

"Slow down," Sara requested. She watched her boys frown, yet they did what she asked and began eating slowly. We mostly sat in silence, exchanging glances at one another, dining, and watching flashes of lightning race across the walls. Thunder shook the room, boom after boom. The sandwiches didn't last long. Daniel laid his napkin on his plate, bounced to his feet, and motioned to take his mother's plate to the kitchen.

"Suck up," Zack barked, shooting his younger brother an evil glance as he grabbed my plate and followed closely behind.

"I wish you didn't have to hurry back to work." I frowned. "At least wait until the weather lets up a little."

Sara gave me a long face; I could tell she didn't want to leave us. I smiled back and gazed into her eyes, trying to convince her we would be fine. Honestly, I was more worried about her driving around in the storm. She wrapped her arms around me and gave me a big hug and a soft kiss. "Drive safe," I whispered. That was the last thing I said before she stood and turned to face the boys as they reentered the room.

"Come here and give your momma a big hug. I need to get back to work," she said as she stretched out her arms, waiting for their embrace. Daniel wasted no time diving into her arms. I smiled with joy, watching the boys with their mother. My mind wandered a bit. *What a wonderful life I have. I married my high school sweetheart and raised two fantastic boys. What more could I ask for?*

"I wish you didn't have to go back to work," Daniel said softly, giving her his pouty face.

"You'll be fine," she reassured him.

I watched Zack hesitate, acting like he was too old for all this mushy stuff. But he was too late as Sara scooped him up in her arms, then gave him one of her giant hugs before planting a huge kiss on his blushing cheeks.

He smirked, trying to pull away. "I'll take care of Dad and Daniel; you have nothing to worry about, Mom."

Sara lowered him to the floor, then turned to me and smiled. I stood and walked her to the front door. She placed her hand on the knob and then slowly turned it. Just as the door opened, she glanced back, shooting me that saucy little smile of hers. "No more ghost stories, John; promise me?"

Shocked, my mouth fell open, and she could see it written all over my face. Why would she think I would tell the boys another ghost story? Okay. She had a point; she's known me all her life. "Alright," I nodded, "we'll play a board game or work on a puzzle or something like that." I grinned. I never said I wouldn't tell the boys another story about Lizardville; honestly, I hadn't finished the first story.

How pathetic am I? I teach my boys the importance of honesty, that your word is all you have. And here I am, showing my boys it is okay to skirt around the truth when necessary. On the flip side, the boys and I were bonding, and that carried more weight. *At least that's my story, and I'm sticking to it.*

Sara gave me that look—the look that said she meant it. I watched as she turned and closed the door, which slammed behind her, making a loud crash. *I don't think she meant to slam the door; it must have been the wind.*

The boys made a beeline for their chairs, and I sat back down in my spot the minute I noticed the headlights roll out of the driveway. The boys stared at me, anxious for me to continue my story. I raised my finger to my chin and took in a deep breath. "So, where was I?" I mumbled.

"You told us that everyone had left the cave, and you never saw the ghost again, or did you?" Zack quizzed me.

"I think you're right..."

I watched Tom return to the small cavern to bury the puzzle box. Shortly after that, we all exited the cave. Buck, Parker, and Todd ensured they covered the entrance so no one would accidentally notice or stumble upon the opening. We wanted to honor Annabelle's wishes and keep Jacob's remains safe. After all, I didn't want to upset Annabelle. She had threatened all of us and looked like a ghost who would honor her word. We were all a little surprised when Jimmy showed up as a ghost. I would have never guessed that, and I wondered why he never showed himself to us before that day. It made sense, though, that he would be a ghost since his death was an accident.

Lexi expressed over and over that this whole experience was super cool. For me, the jury was still out on that subject. I wasn't a hundred percent sure this would be the last time we would see any of them. I often wondered if Jimmy watched over us. Now and then, I would see a door close or a flash out of the corner of my eye, only to look and find no one there. I swear that, occasionally, I would notice things move, too. Maybe Jimmy was having a little fun with me. I could never prove that, but it kept me on my toes.

Even now as an adult, my mind wanders back to that day in the cave. *Are any of the ghosts still around? If they are, what might they be up to these days?* I often asked myself: *Do spirits feel the hot and cold temperatures? Do they sleep? What would it be like to be a ghost?* No, I didn't want to find out. I only wished I had the answers.

"Earth to Dad, are you going to tell us more or not?" Zack's words broke my thoughts.

I looked at the boys sitting wide-eyed in their chairs, just waiting to learn more about my childhood. Okay, maybe not so much about my childhood. Perhaps more about the ghosts I had been telling them about.

"Sorry, I lost my train of thought..." Another bright flash of lightning was followed by another loud crack of thunder rocking the house. This strike was too close for comfort, sending the boys bouncing from their chairs. I have to admit I jumped a little, too. My nerves calmed down. I looked at the boys and remembered the last time I saw Jimmy.

"A year had passed..." I began.

It was 1976, the bicentennial year, two hundred years since the signing of the Declaration of Independence, an important year for our country. The summer was full of events, parades, carnivals, and a mid-summer dance at the volunteer fire station. The township painted the town water tower and fire hydrants red, white, and blue. The United States government had even changed the quarter's design to celebrate the event. I thought the new look was fascinating; that was the day I started collecting coins. Of course, it didn't last long before I spent them when I was short on cash. Who knew that the more money you made, the more you would spend? I still worked several days a week at the general store for Tom Evans, but school and work were my main priorities.

Parker got his driver's license and was driving while my brother, Buck, had received his learner's permit. They both worked at the same gas station in Mill Hall. It was funny how they both worked at the same place and did everything together. The two seemed glued together like a married couple.

Scooter took a job at one of the local restaurants, The Dutch Inn. He washed dishes in the evening and was learning all about the food service business. He was fascinated with food, and I knew he would become a great chef one day. I remember they made the best mouth-watering, cinnamon-flavored sticky buns you could sink your teeth into. Scooter would occasionally bring a few by the house and drop them off on his way home.

Todd had turned to sports and spent much of his time at school with football practice and working out in the gym. He was good and picked up the nickname Tank because he was hard to tackle when he had the football.

Lexi was still working at Burger King. She was saving money for a car and possibly college. She and Buck had dated a few times—it was an off-and-on-again type of friendship. She often talked about getting her degree in paranormal studies—I didn't even know you could get a degree in that.

The summer was over quickly, and the daily life of returning to school hit us in full force. Sara was the youngest and spent most of her time that summer helping her mother around the house while the rest of us were earning money and getting on with our lives. I was unsure what she did all day, though I imagined her reading in a sunny spot because she loved a good book. I would stop over to visit on days I didn't have chores or work, just not as much as I would have liked because of my busy schedule.

The Mill Hall volunteer fire department held several dances a year—it was one of the ways they raised money for new equipment. I learned they had a back-to-school dance at the local fire hall the following Friday. It wasn't anything fancy, just a small dance with a DJ, but it would give me a chance to spend some time with Sara… that's if she wanted to go. No, I didn't care that much for dancing. Who would like to get on the dance floor in front of everyone and make a fool of themselves? I always thought it was odd that the boys would line up along the wall and watch the girls dance. Come to think of it, I guess we were a little strange.

The first day of school came to a close. I stopped by the house to grab a quick bite and then went to the general store. I rode my bike as fast as I could. I still took the trails through the woods that wound along the banks of Big Fishing Creek. It reminded me of the times when Jimmy and I would ride them. I guess that was my way of keeping his memory alive.

I pulled up next to the store like I had done a hundred times before. I had stashed my bike around the back when I noticed a large crow sitting in the tree at the edge of the forest. I took a few steps toward the bird and asked, "Is that you, Annabelle?" I received no response. "Jacob?" Nothing. "Jimmy?" Still nothing, not even a chirp or squawk. I wondered for a minute. I hoped it was him, but still, there was no answer. The crow seemed to follow my every move with his beady eyes. I grew a little frustrated, and I realized it was probably just a crow.

I turned and started to walk toward the front of the store. I needed to remember to ask Tom Evans if I could have next Friday night off to take Sara to the dance. I took a few steps forward before I heard the rustling of the branches behind me and the flapping of wings. I felt a cold chill run down my spine. I turned and spotted the large crow flying toward me. I quickly dropped to the ground and lay flat as possible to avoid being struck. I raised my hands to cover my head as the crow swooped down, brushing my hair. I looked up and watched in disbelief as the crow flew away. *It gave no warning it was going to attack. Why would Annabelle, Jacob, or even Jimmy do that*? Two other crows burst out of the woods and flew in the same direction the first crow had taken; they appeared to be giving chase to the one that attacked me. Odd.

I paused for a second to catch my breath. I couldn't shake the feeling that something was wrong. I bounced to my feet and brushed off my pants before I quickly made my way to the front of the store.

I pushed the door open to the clanging of the bells that hung over it. "Tom," I yelled, "it's just me, Johnny." I didn't want him to think I was a customer, interrupting whatever he was doing. I walked to the closet and grabbed my broom and dustpan just as the office door swung open, startling me for a second.

"Hi, Tom," I blurted out, but he walked past me without saying a word. I thought it was a little odd that he didn't respond. I turned to look, and that's when I noticed he had that look in his eyes—the glazed-over look. His eyes were black, and his face was pale. I had seen this look before when Annabelle stepped into his body. I wasn't sure what to do.

"Are you okay, Mr. Evans?" I asked in a pathetic, soft voice.

I didn't know why, but I was trembling. It wasn't the first time I had seen this look, and the last time Tom didn't attempt to hurt me. Somehow, something appeared different or odd. Tom turned to me. "Get out!" he yelled in a deep voice.

Someone pulled up to the gas pumps, triggering the bells to ring. The sound seemed to snap Tom out of his trance. The color in his eyes slowly returned, and he shook his head slightly. He glanced at me. "Oh, hey, Johnny." He paused for a second. "How long have you been here?"

"I… I just got here," I said.

Tom glanced toward the pumps. "Oh, excuse me. I have a customer," he calmly replied as he strode toward the door. The bells clanged again, and he closed the door behind him as he exited. Just another weird thing that happened today—first, the crow, and now Tom, looking possessed. Could the two be related? I wondered what was going to happen next. I glanced out the front window and saw Old Man Smithers, who stopped at the store quite a bit since he was friends with Tom. You would think that after a year of working at the store, he would have warmed up to me by now, but he hadn't. I shrugged it off; I guess some things will never change.

I watched Tom finish pumping the gas and wash Mr. Smithers' windshield. He collected the money and waved as the old man drove off. The bells clanged as Tom came back inside. "I think someone stepped into my body again," he said, frustrated.

"Why and who?" I asked.

"I wish I knew. I feel helpless when this happens." He paused and shook his head again. "So, how was your day?"

"It was great, thanks. I just finished reading *A Tale of Two Cities*. It's a novel by Charles Dickens, set in London and Paris before and during the French Revolution." Tom loved to read as much as I did, and I thought he would like to know about the story; however, Tom cut me off before I could finish telling him more about the book.

"That's nice." He smiled. "We had a new shipment of canned goods arrive; can you put them on the shelves, please? I'll be in the back room if you need my help." Tom turned and left.

I felt that was a little odd. Tom's never that short with me. He was always cheerful and talkative. Maybe something was weighing on his mind. I put the thought on the back burner for the time being. I turned my attention to unpacking the boxes and placing the cans on the shelf. After restocking, I swept the floors and took out the trash. All I did was clean-up work and odd jobs around his place. Tom never let me help the customers or handle money. Deep down, it made me wonder if he trusted me.

Soon my work was complete, and I found myself back on my bike and almost home when I realized I'd never asked for next Friday off. *I'll have to remember to ask him tomorrow. Hopefully, Tom will be back to his usual self by then.*

# TWO

I didn't have to work the following day, but I made a memorable trip to the store as soon as school let out. I needed to ask Tom if I could have next Friday off. He seemed excited, saying something about young love and all that mushy stuff. I couldn't understand all the fuss. I was only taking my friend Sara to the dance; she just happened to be a girl.

After leaving the store, I climbed on my bike and rode by Sara's house to ask if she would like to go to the dance with me. She was thrilled with the idea and started talking about what dress she would wear and all that jazz.

I tuned her out at that point. I hung out for a bit longer but finally told her I had homework and needed to run home and finish that before the night was over. The remainder of the week and the following week were more like a blur—school and work, work and school, and did I mention all the homework?

The big night finally arrived. The minute I got home from school and walked through the door, Mother was all over me, asking what I would wear. "Jeans and a shirt," I told her. She started acting like Sara had the day I asked her to go with me. Mother became all excited and made a huge deal out of everything. I told her it wasn't like that. It was just two friends going to a dance, which was why I hadn't mentioned to her that I was taking Sara.

After I spent the next hour trying on every piece of clothing I owned, my mother seemed happy with my choice. As we walked to the car, she laid her hand on my shoulder and said what a good-looking guy I was. What an awkward moment, and one I will never forget. I couldn't wait to get to the dance.

With one quick stop to pick up Sara, we would be on our way. Much to my surprise, Mother got out of the car with me when we arrived. Oh, I could tell this was going to be another one of those embarrassing moments, one I would soon regret.

I stepped up to the door, and before I could even raise my hand to knock, the door swung open. Mrs. Parker gazed at me, then smiled, showing all her teeth. "Come in, Johnny." Sara's mom and my mother were acting like two giddy schoolgirls.

"Oh, I can't believe our kids are dating," Mother said.

"I know. Isn't it great?" Mrs. Parker returned. I thought I was going to throw up.

Out of the corner of my eye, I spotted Sara standing at the top of the stairs. Her eyes sparkled. I smiled, and she returned the smile as she glided down the stairs in a beautiful blue dress. "I'm sorry," she mouthed. She could tell how uncomfortable I was with all this girly stuff. It was bad enough that I might have to dance in front of my friends, but I never expected our moms to act this way.

Mrs. Parker grabbed her Polaroid camera. *Oh, great. Pictures.* I noticed Parker smiling at the top of the stairs. His shoulders shook with laughter as he raised his hand to his throat and moved it slightly as if he was choking himself.

Mrs. Parker took a few pictures of Sara and me, then requested my mom be in the picture with us. Next, she asked Mr. Parker to photograph all four of us. He agreed, as long as he didn't have to be in any of them. I guess boys and girls have different opinions about just hanging out, or as our moms wanted to call it, *dating*!

I was growing agitated, so I held my arm out to my side and motioned to Sara. She understood my gesture and laced her arm through mine as we made our way toward the front door. It must have done the trick because our moms slowly followed behind.

I opened the front door for Sara and our mothers. Father had always taught me to be a gentleman, which meant opening the door for the ladies, regardless of age. I think I impressed them from the look on Mother's and Mrs. Parker's faces.

As we crossed the porch and descended the stairs, making our way toward the car, I noticed a single large crow watching us from the trees. I could just see it out of the corner of my eye. The bird's eyes followed our every step. *Please don't attack. Please don't attack.* From the look on Sara's face, I think she shared the same feeling.

The crow continued to gawk at us as I opened the car door for Sara. I walked to the other side and sat in the back seat beside her. I felt a little relieved that the crow never moved. It didn't take long before Sara rolled down the rear window. "Excuse me, can we go, please?" She smiled, and I think they both got the hint. Mother climbed into the car, and with a slight wave to Sara's mom, we were off. I couldn't help but notice as we pulled out that the crow had taken flight. I hoped it would not follow us to the fire hall. This night was supposed to be fun, and I didn't want to have to deal with the supernatural.

It took a few minutes before the car slowed, and we pulled into the fire hall. As the car stopped, I opened the door, bounced out, and headed to the other side. But Sara was already halfway out before I could open the door. I guess she wanted to escape from my mom as fast as possible.

I glanced over to Mother. "See you at eleven." I smiled, and she nodded as the car turned and drove out of sight.

Sara and I were finally alone. A wave of relief flooded over us. We turned and made our way toward the entrance. You could hear the music blasting, and the wall appeared to be vibrating. Sara glanced to the right and then pointed toward the upper corner of the roof. A single crow sat watching us, and we picked up our pace to the front door. I was already a little jittery; I didn't need the crow upsetting our first date. Since everyone else was calling it a date, I might as well, too.

I shrugged my shoulders, acting like it was no big deal. I guess I was playing the tough guy routine. "It's just a coincidence." I smiled.

Once inside, it was just like I thought—all the girls were on the dance floor, and the guys stayed huddled on the far side of the room. I spotted Todd and Scooter—I didn't even know they were coming. After looking around, I figured most of the kids in town were here. Sara and I made our way over to the table, and I grabbed us two glasses of punch. Slowly, I inched us in the direction of the guys—I didn't know what else to do. Call it being shy or just silly.

Sara noticed a few of her friends from school and excused herself to the dance floor. Great news for me. I made a beeline for Todd and Scooter. "Hey guys, what's up?" I asked.

Todd nodded as Scooter replied, "Hey, man, I didn't know you were coming."

"I could say the same thing," I answered. "It's great to see you both."

"I see you brought Sara," Todd said.

"Yeah, she's pretty cool." I smiled.

"I think you like her," Scooter jabbed.

My face turned a little red. "I do."

It wasn't much of a first date. I hung out with the guys for a while and watched Sara dance from afar. From time to time, she'd glance in my direction and smile, almost like a gesture asking if it was okay that she continued to dance. I was happy with that. After all, I didn't want to embarrass myself. Suddenly, a sharp pain shot through my stomach and then another. I didn't know what was happening, but I knew something was wrong. Maybe it was from all the adult chaperones who were smoking.

"Whoa, wait a minute, Dad; you can't smoke in a public place," Daniel smirked.

"Well, this was the 70s. People were allowed to smoke almost anywhere they wanted back then." I frowned.

"Really?" Zack chimed.

"It's true," I explained. "A lot of things have changed since the 70s, some for the better and others not so much,"

I smirked as I watched the boys relax. Since the boys had no more questions, I continued with my story.

A sharp pain stabbed my side. I applied pressure with my hand with little success. My head started to spin, and I decided to get some fresh air. I excused myself and made my way to the door. The fireman tending the door asked if I was coming back in, and I replied, "yes." I held out my right hand and watched him stamp it with a black ink marker so I could reenter the dance. It never occurred to me to tell Sara that I was stepping out.

I pushed my way through the cars in the parking lot. I walked in the direction of Fishing Creek, which briskly flowed past, and I trudged my way to the top of the dike. Dikes surrounded the town of Mill Hall to help prevent flooding, which worked most of the time, but not always. I turned and looked back at the fire hall some twenty feet below and could still hear the music playing.

I stood on the top, looking at the moonlight reflecting off the water. The light glittered as the water rushed past—it was so peaceful. I was about to sit down when I heard a crow squawk. I looked around but didn't see anything. It cawed louder and louder, and then I noticed a splash in the water. I turned my head back and forth, trying to see if it was a crow that had entered the water. *I must be hearing or seeing things.* I realized it must have been a fish jumping out, trying to catch an insect.

Then a faint light appeared in the water. I blinked a few times and rubbed my eyes with my hands. This couldn't be real—the light was growing. I looked back over the bank toward the fire hall. I guess I was the only person around. I looked back toward the water and watched as a ghostly white vapor began to take the shape of a person. It reminded me of the day I had opened the puzzle box when it emitted a stream of light and gas. But we had buried the box in the cave next to Jacob's body. Yet, a similar bright light was glowing in the middle of the creek.

I watched as it started to move in my direction, brighter and brighter, the glare almost blinding. It continued to grow and was nearly double its original size. This wasn't the first time I had seen a ghost, and I was sure it wouldn't be the last. My mind raced to Annabelle, but what could she want from me? Had something happened to Jimmy?

Even though Jimmy and I used to hang out, I still struggled to wrap my head around the fact that my best friend was a ghost. Then it became clear that it wasn't her; it was Jimmy gliding toward me. It appeared as if he was walking on water. I couldn't believe it: I was face to face with a ghost again.

As he drew closer, I could see he was upset. "What's wrong?" I asked.

He rambled on, talking faster than I could comprehend. He glanced at me and then softly said, "Everything, just everything." He looked like he was ready to cry.

"Slow down, Jimmy. I can't understand what you're saying."

He stopped, took a deep breath, and gazed into my eyes. "Jacob's gone."

"What? How could that be?" I was confused. None of this made sense.

"One minute, Annabelle, Jacob, and I were sitting near the dam, watching a few guys fishing. Then the next thing

I know, Annabelle let out a loud scream. She was pissed. I turned and saw her glare fixed on Jacob. I spun to look back to Jacob and watched him evaporate before my eyes. It only took a few seconds, and he vanished like that." Jimmy tried to click his thumb and finger together to make a clicking sound, but I heard nothing.

He continued, "Then I watched in disbelief as Annabelle collapsed. She cried and cried. Then her sadness turned to anger. I didn't know what to say or do. I wasn't even sure what was going on; it was crazy. And then she changed into a crow and flew away. I haven't seen her in days. I'm scared, alone, and cursed."

Speechless, I looked at Jimmy.

His eyes were fixed on mine as he shook his head. A minute had passed before I raised my hands, still not knowing how to respond. "Wait," I blurted out. "Are you saying Jacob is gone?"

Jimmy shook his head from side to side. He wasn't sure, but it looked that way.

"Is he gone forever? Is that what you're saying?"

"I think so..." He seemed uncertain.

"Did someone go to the cave and tamper with his body?" I asked.

Jimmy looked at me in silence for a few seconds. "It's possible. I didn't think of that," he replied.

"That's the first thing we need to check out." The detective side of me was kicking in. "How do I contact you when I need you?"

He stared at me and said, "I'll be in touch with you like I summoned you today." It was then that I realized my stomach was feeling better. I heard the scuffling of feet coming up behind me. I turned my head and noticed Sara walking toward me.

"There you are. Why didn't you tell me you were leaving? I felt scared. I thought I did something to upset you." She cast a nervous look at me.

"I'm sorry if I frightened you. I just needed some fresh air, and it looked like you were having a good time dancing. So, I decided not to disturb you." I paused. "It was weird… I had this feeling come over me, and it pulled me in the direction of the creek. That's when Jimmy appeared, and he and I have been talking," I spun my head and pointed toward Jimmy. Sara looked, but he was already gone.

"I don't see anyone," she said, casting a look of doubt.

"I swear, he was right here. He's upset and needs our help," I said. I brought her up to speed, explaining every-thing Jimmy had told me. "Oh my," was the only reaction I got from Sara. She brought up some good points. "Why would anyone go up there? There were only a few of us that even knew of the location of the cave. And who would want the remains?"

My mind raced to Tom Evans—he was the obvious choice. But why would he want to go back? Could it be that he wanted the puzzle box back? But he gave us his word. The second person that came to mind was Old Man Smithers. But how would he even know about the place? Unless he and Tom were in on this together. But why would Tom want to bring harm to Annabelle? After all, she was his great-great-grandmother. Something wasn't adding up.

We both knew what we needed to do. We had to get the group back together and hike to the top of the mountain. I had to know for sure, and I could tell Sara felt the same way. I grabbed her hand, and she smiled. We made our way down the embankment and were just about to set foot in the parking lot when Mr. Fienberg noticed us. Just when I thought this night couldn't get worse, it did. That's one of the problems of living in a small town. Everyone knows who you are.

Mr. Fienberg, a teacher from school, was chaperoning the dance. He had a reputation around school that he'd make you pay the price if you broke the rules. I didn't even know he would be here tonight. *Great*, I thought.

"Stop, both of you," he hollered. "Sara, what on earth are you doing out here? Why were you on the other side of the bank with this… this boy?"

"We were only talking," she tried to explain.

"Well, you both know the rules. Now I have to detain you and call your parents. Let's see what they have to say about this," he smirked.

"You don't understand, Mr. Fienberg. We were—" I tried to say more, but he cut me off before I could finish.

"Hush," he yelled and pointed at the two of us. I'm sure he was feeling like a big man now.

I turned to Sara and mouthed the word, "Sorry."

She nodded in return. The frown on her face told me she would be in trouble for leaving the dance, but I felt confident that once our moms arrived, things would be fine. After all, they were so giddy about us going on this date.

It didn't take long for my mom and Mrs. Parker to arrive. I thought they were going to rip my head off. "What were you thinking, sneaking off to be alone with Sara? You should be ashamed of yourself! Do you have anything to say?" Mother barked.

This was not going the way I expected. Before I could even open my mouth, Mrs. Parker started yelling at me.

"Did you touch my daughter? She's only thirteen. What were you thinking?"

Sara quickly jumped up and barked, "We didn't do anything, Mom!"

The bickering lasted a few minutes before the ladies escorted Sara and me to the car. I sat as far away from Sara as possible. It hurt that she wouldn't even look at me. I tried to reach out, but my mother turned and waved her finger in my face. I bowed and slightly shook my head. *What a disaster. First, Jimmy was hurting and needed my help, and I couldn't do anything. And now, Sara won't even look at me.*

I had only stepped outside to get some fresh air. Now Sara and I were in trouble for leaving the dance. Could this night get any worse?

The minute we got home, I received my answer. Father grounded me for a week. And then, to make matters worse, he explained how you need to respect women and started talking about the birds and the bees. *Yuck.*

"Don't even think about having that talk with me." Zack chuckled.

Daniel looked on, his mouth hanging open. I thought he was going to say something, but he didn't. I could tell by the look in his eye that he was taken aback by the conversation.

# THREE

That was the longest week of my life. Wake up, go to school, and then go back home, only to be confined to my bedroom. When you think back to 1976, we didn't even have the electronics the kids have today. There was nothing in my room—no TV, phone, or video games. The only thing I could do was homework and read. I had the chance to finish a few books. Since I liked a good story, I guess it wasn't all that bad.

I was livid when I learned that Mr. Evans agreed with my parents. Who was he to enforce my punishment? That raised my suspicion that he might be involved in some way. Why didn't he want me at the store? My mind whirled with ideas—none of them good. Things weren't adding up. Why would he want to hurt Annabelle? Wasn't she his great-great-grandmother? I knew I'd get to the bottom of this. All I needed was a little help. And being grounded gave me time to think about what Jimmy had told me. I was already hatching a plan.

Since today was my last day of being grounded and tomorrow was the start of the weekend, I figured we should get the gang together. I spoke with Buck, and he arranged everything. We would all meet at Parker's house around eight. *Man, this trip is going to bring back memories.* I finished dinner and went straight to my room. Taking notes and studying the encyclopedia, I was learning more about the paranormal world than I ever thought possible. I added that to what I already knew—the stuff that couldn't be found in any of these books. The books never mentioned that a ghost could turn into a crow. *What if they can turn into something else, like a mountain lion?* The thought alone sent a shiver up my spine.

Hearing footsteps on the stairs, I closed my notepad and the book and slid them under my bed. The door slowly creaked open. I noticed it was only Buck. "Oh, it's you."

"Nice to see you too," Buck snapped. It wasn't easy sharing a bedroom with my older brother.

"That was not what I meant. I was researching paranormal stuff and didn't want Mom or Dad to find out what I was looking at. I'm glad it was only you." I smiled and watched Buck drop onto his bed.

"Can't you talk like a normal person?" Buck asked.

I was a little dumbfounded by the question. "What do you mean?"

"You know, words like *paranormal*. A normal person would say *ghost stuff*."

"Oh, okay, I guess," I smirked and climbed into bed.

"Lights out," he barked. I watched as the room fell into darkness.

Morning came quickly for us. I didn't think I would sleep well, but much to my surprise, I did. The sun beamed through the curtains, and I bounced out of bed. I slipped on my pants and slid the T-shirt over my head. Next, I added a long sleeve flannel shirt, grabbed my lightweight blue jacket, and went downstairs to the bathroom. I brushed my teeth and grabbed a banana before walking toward the front door. Buck was only a few steps behind me, carrying the small backpack that contained a few supplies.

Buck and I didn't say much as we walked toward Parker's house. I glanced his way a few times, but I wasn't able to read his expression. Maybe he wasn't fully awake; I didn't know. But the silence was bothering me. I tossed the banana peel over the guardrail into the weeds.

I glanced around the house. It was nice to see the whole gang. Scooter stood in the corner wearing a bright red hunting jacket. *Wow* was my first impression. *You could see that jacket from a mile away*. No one was going to mistake him for a deer in the forest. I was sure Jimmy and Annabelle wouldn't miss him, either. I assumed they were going to make an appearance at the cave. Parker was wearing his camouflage jacket and black pants. I snickered because Buck was wearing the same thing.

Todd wore his black high school letterman jacket with a large white B on the front. The B stood for B.E.N., short for Bald Eagle Nittany High School. Even though he was a jock, I was glad Todd never forgot about his camping buddies.

I spotted Lexi filling some canteens with Sara by her side in the kitchen. Lexi wore a lovely pink jacket and skin-tight jeans—she always stayed up with the latest fashion trends. Sara was dressed in a plain brown coat and blue jeans. It felt like she was avoiding me. I guess she was still mad at me for getting her into trouble. I didn't blame her for that—I didn't enjoy getting punished, either. *Oh well,* nothing I can do about that now. I needed to stay focused and see what we could do to help Jimmy.

Something was wrong—the excitement level was missing. I wasn't looking forward to the climb either, but it was something we had to do. I was happy that everyone at least showed up—except for Tom Evans, but we didn't invite him.

"Can I have everyone's attention, please?" Parker shouted.

The room fell silent. Parker warned us about the risk we were taking. Hunting season was near, and we could run into a hunter or two on the trail. He added that the brush would be thinner this time of year, offering us less coverage.

"Just get on with it, will you? I think we all know the risks," Lexi retorted as she turned and headed toward the door. Sara spun on her heels and followed her outside. I don't know why that surprised me, as I could tell she had this little attitude thing happening.

"Why not?" I laughed and followed the girls, and Scooter did the same. I exited the door, letting it slam behind me, and spotted the girls, who had already made their way across the yard and were starting up the mountain trail. The cold morning air tickled my nose.

"Wait up, dude," Scooter said as he jogged to catch up.

"Sorry, trying to keep up with Lexi and Sara. I guess they want to get this over with." I frowned. In the back of my mind, I hoped to find Jimmy, Annabelle, and Jacob at the top of the mountain. However, this nagging little feeling told me that would not happen.

I heard Todd, Buck, and Parker complain behind us about Lexi taking off as she did. *For once, they are not leading the way*, I thought.

A half hour had passed, and you could tell the forest was in winter mode—empty branches on trees and shrubs offered little or no hiding place. The seven of us pushed on toward the top. The cracking sound of branches and dried leaves under our feet engulfed us.

Lexi pushed onward and upward like a girl on a mission, not even stopping for a break. I started to recognize some of the surroundings. *We must be getting close.* The little stream that crossed the path and the distant rock formations brought back memories. The air was much colder, and the leaves were all missing from the trees, except for the pine trees, and there were plenty of them around. My mind fast-forwarded to Christmas, thinking we might come up here and cut down our tree. I jerked my head around at the sound of a crow squawking. It quickly brought me back to reality. The group came to a stop. Heads turned in all directions, and we were all unsure which direction the sound had come from.

Branches snapped and fell as a large crow broke through the trees, followed by two more. I swear it looked like those two were chasing the first crow. *Could that be Annabelle, Jacob, and Jimmy? Could it be someone else, someone we had never met before?* I immediately knew something wasn't right, and my stomach was tied in knots. I galloped ahead of the others, running at a light pace. I didn't care if they followed; I needed to see what was in the cave.

I huffed and puffed, trying to catch my breath, but kept my feet moving onward and upward. I spotted the overhanging cliff and heard water dripping into a large pond. I pushed and shoved my way through the overgrown brush and burst into the clearing. I froze where I stood. The pool of water was blood red. What happened to the crystal-clear blue water that was here a year ago?

Parker, Buck, Sara, and Lexi showed up behind me, and Scooter arrived momentarily. They paused and looked.

"Why'd you take off, dude?" Scooter questioned, gasping for breath.

I turned toward him. "I had this bad feeling, and I was right. The pond's filled with blood," I gasped. I faced Sara and Lexi, who seemed perfectly calm. I turned back to Scooter, then glanced at Parker and Buck. No one seemed as shocked as I was.

"What are you talking about?" Parker asked.

I glanced back at the pool of water, which was crystal clear. I shook my head, closed my eyes, and reopened them. I didn't imagine it. At least, I was pretty sure I didn't. A loud squawking sound came from the top of the falls. The sound of several birds followed; the large crow took off, followed by a smaller one. A second later, a large crow stepped to the front of the cliff, gazing down at us with his beady, red eyes. Did the crow turn the water red for me? An eerie feeling fell over me, and I sprinted toward the cave. The crow cawed louder and louder; I felt he was telling us this was his mountain, and it was time for us to go. But I wasn't leaving until I had some answers.

I pushed my way toward the opening, tossing branches to the side. Parker, Todd, and Buck quickly joined in. Everyone had the same notion—get inside the cave where it was safe. We squeezed through the tight space one by one—the girls and even Scooter followed.

"How do we keep that thing out?" Parker asked as he flicked on his flashlight.

Todd grabbed a few branches and tried to block the entrance the best he could. I had a terrible feeling they would not be enough to keep the birds out. *Why would Annabelle act like this? Was it her? Was she mad because Jacob was gone?* My mind raced for answers that I didn't have. I gazed down the dark tunnel. "Are we ready?" I motioned and started my descent.

Sara started to whimper. I turned and watched Lexi put her arm around her. Another flashlight flicked on, and Parker joined me as we trudged forward, going deeper into the cave. We came to the area where the floor sloped down. It was damp and very slippery this time. Leaning back, I stepped forward and placed one foot on the slope. The minute my foot hit the slick section, I lost my balance, landed on my butt, and slid down the fifteen feet to the bottom. I caught myself just in time before I fell forward. "I'm okay," I hollered back. Buck and Todd decided to stay up top in case we needed help getting back up.

Parker was the next to slide down, and Lexi was on his heels. "I think that's all of us," she said. I guess the rest of them were staying topside. I didn't have time to think about it. I turned and headed to the hidden room we had found the year before on the left side of the cavern wall.

Ten, maybe twenty, yards further, and we would be standing outside the opening. I took a deep breath, hoping to see the ground the way we had left it a year ago. "Are we ready?" I asked Parker and Lexi. They both nodded. Part of me wanted to enter the room, but another part of me didn't want to move. I swallowed and felt a shiver run down my spine, my heart pounding. Was this what a heart attack felt like?

Screaming and screeching resonated in the cavern. The sounds were coming from behind. I thought of Sara. *Would she be alright*? I knew Todd and Buck wouldn't let anything happen to her. I relaxed a bit, took a deep breath, and stepped through the entryway of the smaller room. Parker's flashlight beamed around the room as he and Lexi followed. I knew we had to be quick. The noises behind us in the cave sounded horrible, and I feared for my friends. The squawking sounded more agitated, and I thought I heard Sara whimper, followed by Todd and Buck reassuring her that we would be quick. I shook my head; I needed to concentrate.

Parker moved the light from left to right and finally back in the corner. I gasped at the large pile of dirt and the size of the hole next to it—deep and empty. "What the heck," I whispered. I turned to face Lexi, and her hand covered her mouth, a stunned expression on her face. Parker's jaw hung open. *Who could have done this? Who else knew about this place? And why hadn't we heard anything in town about the discovery of a body?* This would have been big news for the small towns of Lizardville and Mill Hall.

Too many questions loomed, and I still had no answers. I was flabbergasted. Jimmy was right—something had happened. The sound of the crows squawking grew louder, and I knew we didn't have time to stick around and investigate. Parker, Lexi, and I turned and dashed for the opening in the wall. I could tell the others were struggling with something or someone. I wanted to run in the other direction, but that would send me deeper into the cave. We had never gone beyond this point. Would it be safe? I spotted Parker and Lexi hunkered down at the base of the wall, and I decided to do the same as a large crow and a smaller crow appeared out of nowhere.

They flew at one another, colliding with their claws drawn. It was too dark to see much, and I only caught a glimpse here and there as to who was winning. Squawking and crying sounds filled the cavern as another crow came into view, making it two-on-one from what I could tell. But who were they, and why were they fighting? Suddenly, the smaller one slammed into the wall and fell close to my feet. A second crow slammed into the wall on the other side of the cavern, and the largest bird took flight and vanished.

Amazed, I looked at the crow at my feet. It started to glow and transform, and soon I saw Jimmy. He looked hurt, knocked out or something. "Jimmy," I yelled and crawled next to him. I reached to lay a hand on his shoulder, but it passed straight through him.

He blinked and stared up at me. "I'm fine," he whispered.

"That didn't go well," a woman's voice chimed in.

"Annabelle!" I shouted. She froze and gazed back.

I couldn't believe it. Both of them were here. Lexi and Parker remained silent, leaning against the wall. "Where's Jacob?" I blurted out, not even thinking about what Jimmy had told me. Annabelle's eyes flared, and she screamed and vanished in a vicious rage before our eyes. I spun and looked at Jimmy. "I'm sorry…" He nodded slightly, and I sighed. "I guess I upset her by mentioning Jacob."

"She'll be fine."

"Are you alright?"

"I just got the crap knocked out of me. What do you think?"

I smiled. "You look alright to me. How many fingers am I holding up?" I asked, holding up three fingers.

He grinned. "All of them."

I smiled back, knowing he was pulling my leg. "Can ghosts get hurt?" I asked.

"Yes and no. I'm not sure I can die since I'm already dead." He chuckled. "I feel drained if that makes any sense." He smiled and laughed a little more.

"If Jacob vanished, then who were you and Annabelle fighting?"

Jimmy frowned. "That was Donald Thornhill…" He paused. "Do you remember the story Parker told us at the campfire? He explained that the ax factory owner killed Jacob and hid his body in this cave. Donald was mean and nasty, and he was also Annabelle's husband. Remember, Annabelle told you to stay away from him. She was right. After Jacob evaporated—or crossed over as you would call it—Annabelle mourned, but then she got angry and went after Donald. Things have been crazy ever since. Now she wants revenge."

My mouth dropped open. Lexi and Parker moved closer so they could hear Jimmy's story. "So, how can we help?" I asked.

"I'm not sure…" He frowned. "I wish I could cross over and move on. Then Annabelle and Donald could fight it out. But deep down, I feel like I owe her something."

"You owe her nothing, Jimmy. She took your life," I blurted out, noticing my voice getting loud. Jimmy's face went blank, and his lip quivered a bit. "I'm sorry; I didn't mean it like that. I care about you, man. I mean, we all care about you and only you."

"Thanks," he smiled back, "but I must help her. I mean, yes, I want to cross over, but I think if I help her, maybe I can move on, too."

I nodded my head in agreement. "How can we help?" He wasn't sure, so I told him I would research and ask Tom Evans if he knew anything about Jacob's disappearance. We both knew I was grasping at straws. What would it take to help Jimmy cross over? I needed to dig deep, maybe go to the library and see their books on the supernatural.

"Jimmy, we need to head back down the mountain. I need to come up with a plan. I need answers." I noticed Lexi nod in agreement.

"I can take you to the library," Lexi offered. "Maybe we can find something to help us understand what needs to be done."

"That would be great." Jimmy sighed. "You should go. I'll be in touch. Stay safe, my friends."

Then it hit me. "Wait… how do we find you?"

"I'll give you a few days and then stop by your house to talk."

Lexi and I smiled. "That sounds great." Parker agreed, and before I could say goodbye, Jimmy was gone.

# FOUR

**W**asting no time, Parker stretched out his hand and helped me. Lexi, Parker, and I started back toward the cave entrance. As we approached the slippery incline, Parker yelled to get Buck and Todd's attention. "We need to get a running start up the slope, so be ready to grab us before we slide back down."

"You got it; we're ready!" Buck replied as he, Scooter, and Todd joined hands to form a human chain. They lowered themselves part of the way down the rock surface. "Ready."

That's all I needed to hear, and I took off running, hitting the slope at full speed. I took several steps before I started to lose traction; the rocks were wetter than I expected. I extended my hand and missed Buck's by a few inches. I slowly drifted backward until I hit bottom. I backed up a little farther to give myself room to gain momentum. Once again, I hit the ground running, but this time I extended my hand and found Buck's. Our fingers interlocked, my feet still sliding forward, and then he wrapped his hand around mine and pulled me to the top. Parker ran next, his long legs helping him quickly scale the slippery surface. Sara shined the light back down, and Lexi promptly followed, making her way up the slope.

"Well?" Buck asked.

"Well, what?" I said.

"Don't be a butt. You know what I mean. Was everything okay? Was the body still there?"

Before I could chime in, Lexi replied, "All we found was an empty hole in the ground."

"Well crap, what about the puzzle box?"

I had forgotten all about the box. *Should we go back and try to find it?* Before I could finish my thought, Parker answered, "What's it matter? If the body's gone, who cares about the box?"

"I agree," said Lexi.

I nodded in agreement, and so did the others. We turned and made our way toward the entrance. I filled Scooter in on what happened at the gravesite—that we talked with Jimmy and that Annabelle even made a brief appearance. Scooter mentioned that the crows buzzed past so quickly that none of them had a chance to see or do anything. What concerned us most was this Donald Thornhill character. Who was he? And what was his story? I blurted out to Lexi that maybe we could find out more about him at the library. After all, he owned the ax factory and was an essential person in his era.

The seven of us continued our trek to the entrance of the cave. The outside light grew brighter as we approached. One by one, we exited and gathered around the little pond. I sat on an old fallen log, and Scooter took a spot next to me. "When are you going to the library?"

"I don't know. That depends on Lexi."

"I would like to go today if you have nothing else to do," she said.

I nodded in agreement. Sara sent a bit of a nasty look my way. *Was she jealous of her sister? Good,* I thought. I faced Scooter, and the two of us chatted, though I wasn't sure I was listening as he rambled on about not much of anything. My mind drifted to Jimmy and his wanting to cross over. How could we make that happen? What would happen to Annabelle and Donald Thornhill? I was eager to get off this mountain, and from the look on Lexi's face, so was she. She stood and motioned with her head. I got to my feet, and so did the others, seemingly without a thought or care in the world. We looked like a bunch of string puppets, where someone would pull the cords to make them stand, sit, or walk. I chuckled to myself. "What's so funny?" Sara blurted out.

I snapped out of my daze. "Nothing, just thinking about how this was the second time we've had a run-in with ghosts."

She smirked, pivoted, and made her way to the bushes surrounding the pond and then vanished into the foliage. The walk home was long and uneventful. Sometimes I felt like something was watching us—an extra set of eyes keeping tabs on us. A few times, I stopped and looked around. It was calm yet eerie, and it felt like something wasn't quite right. Then it registered—there were no sounds, only the sound of our footsteps. It was quiet, too quiet if you asked me. Could all the animals be sleeping or hiding from us? I guess that the animals knew enough to stay away. Something lurked in the woods. They knew it, and so did I.

Parker's house came into view, and I smiled, knowing we were safe—time to dig in and do some research. But my hopes were dashed since Lexi wasn't allowed to use the car. Her mother had to run some errands, and she didn't have the time to drop us off at the library, so our answers would have to wait. Parker, Buck, and Todd grabbed their fishing gear and hit the creek one last time before winter arrived. Sara and Lexi had chores to finish, leaving Scooter and me … until he dropped a bomb on me. "Dude, I need to be heading home. I told my mom I wouldn't be gone too long." I bounced on the balls of my feet a few times and clicked my tongue. I didn't want to waste the day, and I had already read through the encyclopedias at our house. I doubted I would find anything new. I started hatching a new idea. I said my goodbyes and walked home.

The minute I pushed the door open and tossed my jacket onto the couch, I heard Mother yell at me to take out the trash. *Ugh*. "I thought it was Buck's turn," I shouted back. Then I heard Father yell, "Do as your mother asked."

"Yes, sir," I responded, grabbing the bag and going to the trash can.

I slammed the metal lid down with a clash, letting the world know how frustrated I was with doing Buck's chores. I don't think the world cared if I liked it, though. Then a thought tugged at my mind—I wasn't grounded anymore. I bounced in the door and yelled that I was going to the general store to see if Tom needed help. It was time to get back to work, and this would allow me to see if he knew anything about Jacob or had anything to do with what had happened.

"Okay, but don't be too late," Mother hollered from the kitchen.

I had permission to go, so I darted out the door, grabbed my bike, and peddled as fast as possible. The cool fall breeze slapped me in the face—I should have grabbed my jacket, but it was too late now. Moments later, I slammed on the brakes, skidded to a stop, tossed my bike behind the store, and skipped to the front. The bells above the door chimed as I made my way through. "Tom, are you here?" I bellowed.

"Back here," he replied from his office.

As I pushed the door open, I spotted Tom sitting in the corner on his old chair, his head buried in a book. "Hey, what are you reading?"

"Oh, nothing much," he replied, laying the book on the little table. "So, what brings you to the store today? I wasn't expecting to see you until tomorrow."

"I know this is a bit unexpected, but I have to ask you some questions."

Tom smiled. "Sure, fire away."

"I saw Jimmy over a week ago at the fire hall dance—that was why I was outside. It didn't have anything to do with Sara." Tom looked at me, giving me an understanding smile. I could tell by the look on his face that he believed me, and I think he felt terrible for not believing me in the first place. That's the kind of friendship Tom and I had developed over the past year. I liked and trusted him, even though he was an adult. That meant a lot to me.

"Jimmy said Jacob crossed over, vanished, poof, gone… you know what I mean?"

Tom gave me a puzzled look and blinked a few times. I guess he was trying to comprehend what I was saying. His mouth opened, then closed, then opened again before he finally asked, "How…? I mean, when?"

*I didn't think to ask Jimmy.* "I guess Jacob's been gone a few weeks since he told me the night of the dance. After that, Father grounded me, so yes, I would guess two, maybe three weeks. Why? Does that matter?"

The puzzled look was still on his face. He glanced at me a few times. I guess he was searching for the right words to say. "I'm a bit confused," he finally replied.

"Anyway, there's more," I added. "We all gathered this morning and hiked up the mountain to see if anything had happened to Jacob's grave."

Tom leaned forward in his chair, elbows on his knees. "Why would you go to the site?"

"I thought if something happened to his grave … like it was dug up, it could cross him over." I paused.

"Well, that makes sense," he said.

"When we arrived, all we found was a giant hole and no body." I studied Tom's reaction, and it looked like he was examining me. I don't think either of us knew what to make of it.

"What about the puzzle box? Was it gone?" Tom asked.

"You're the second person to ask me about the box. I didn't look since we were interrupted. Three crows showed up, and things got crazy from then on, squawking and fighting. We couldn't wait to get out of there."

"What do you mean the second person to ask? Who else did you tell?"

"No one. When we were on our way back, Parker asked if the box was there. That's when I realized I didn't take the time to look. But, if you let me continue, I can tell you one of the crows was Jimmy, and another was Annabelle. We talked briefly, but Jimmy said the other crow was Donald Thornhill." I paused, trying to remember more details. Tom bit his lip and looked remorseful. *Had he done something wrong?* "Did you take the body?" I asked sharply.

Shock riveted his face. "What? Me? No way. Why would I do that?"

"It's just that look on your face. You seem guilty or something."

"I wouldn't want to hurt any of them; Annabelle is my great-great-grandmother. I wouldn't hurt her." His eyes were saddened, cast downward to the floor.

"Then why the face? You look like you know something. Did you tell someone?" I demanded.

"No…" his voice trailed off as he thought about it for a minute. "Wait, I did tell Bob Smithers. But he's a dear friend—"

"Why would you tell anyone?" I interrupted. I felt betrayed yet confident. I didn't think I was rude by asking these questions, even though Tom was an adult. I was sure Tom understood my position and how I felt since everything that happened affected Jimmy.

"I'm sorry. I felt like I could trust him. I sure hope I didn't cause any of this. Do you know what I mean? Jacob crossing over." He looked disappointed. "Help me clean up the shop, and I'll close early today. Then I'll drive over and visit Bob to see if he told anyone or if he went up to the site himself."

I smiled. "You would do that? Wow, that would be great." Another idea flooded my mind. "Hey, can I use your phone to call my mom?"

"Sure, no problem." He pushed his chair back and slowly made his way out into the store.

Quickly, I grabbed the phone and began to dial Scooter's number. "Oh, please be home," I whispered. Scooter's mom answered. Oh yes, I was in luck; he was home. We talked for a few minutes, and he agreed to meet me at Old Man

Smithers' in half an hour. I knew he would wait, even if I were a little late. We had to find out what those two men were up to.

After hanging up the phone, I grabbed the trash and swept the floors as quickly as possible. My emotions were overflowing with excitement. It felt like a thousand butterflies were churning inside me. In no time at all, I was finished. "See you tomorrow, and let me know what you find out," I told Tom and bolted for the door. With some luck, I could get there before Tom showed up. I grabbed my bike and headed for the mountain trail—it was a shortcut. The ride only took about ten minutes before I found myself at the edge of Old Man Smithers' property. Dusk was setting in, and the moon reflected across his lawn. I spotted Scooter sitting on the stump, waiting for me.

We stayed hidden in the trees, but we knew we needed to get closer so we could listen to what the two men had to say. "Thanks for coming," I whispered as I stashed my bike in the high weeds.

"No problem. What's so urgent that you dragged me out here tonight?" Scooter asked.

He seemed a little nervous, and he had every right to be. If we got caught, all hell would break loose. I could lose my job, and Scooter could get grounded. Oh crap, I could get grounded, too; that was the last thing I needed. I filled him in on what Tom and I had discussed at the store. He felt the same way I did, and I told him that was why I didn't call the others. They would have blown up, and we needed to be in stealth mode to find out the truth.

A set of headlights appeared on the opposite side of the field, and I was sure Tom had arrived. "Come on. Follow me." I waved a hand for Scooter to follow. I started to trot with Scooter right on my heels. We pushed our way through the tall weeds as we inched closer to the house. We stopped, and I pointed to a tree about twenty yards ahead on the freshly-cut grass.

The lights went out on Tom's car. I watched as he exited and walked up the gravel driveway. I knew the crunching of the rocks would mask any noise we would make. Our chance had arrived; we needed to go undetected. We made a break for it, stopping at the first tree and then dashing for the next tree a little closer to the house. I lay down on the grass and began crawling toward the house. I could feel the coolness of the ground against my stomach. Thank goodness the dew hadn't started to form yet.

We cautiously approached, inching closer to the window. I could see the light shine over the grass as the front door opened and closed. I crawled faster. I didn't want to miss anything. Then I heard Scooter whisper, "What about the dog?" I had forgotten all about his dog.

"With a little luck, the dog will be asleep," I mumbled, trying to be optimistic. We inched closer and closer until we were right under the large bay window on the left side of the house. I could hear the two men talking, but I wasn't close enough to listen to what they were saying. I partially stood up and rested my ear right next to the bottom of the window. I was in luck—the window was slightly cracked open to allow a breeze in the house. I could hear every word.

"Well, Tom, I'm surprised to see you here this evening."

"Oh, you know, I closed up shop a bit early so I could see how you were doing,"

It sounded like Tom was a bit nervous. I hoped he wouldn't tip his hand and make things worse for Jimmy. Many thoughts raced through my mind. *Why would Tom tell Old Man Smithers about the cave? Was he into that sort of thing? Dead bodies? Maybe the old man just liked mysteries? None of this made sense.* I pressed my ear tightly to the bottom of the glass. I was thankful the curtains were closed.

"I don't think you stopped to just check on me." The old man sounded suspicious. "Why don't you tell me why you're here?"

Tom took a long pause. I was beginning to wonder if he was even going to answer him.

"Do you hear something?" Scooter whispered. Startled, I flinched a little, and my head slightly banged against the window. I panicked and ducked down to the grass as we pressed ourselves tightly to the house while trying to stay low to the ground. Moments passed, maybe a minute, and we heard nothing. I guess they didn't hear us. Perhaps I was paranoid, that jittery feeling settling back in my stomach as I slowly rose back up to the window. I poked my head up and looked through the glass. The dog was looking out the window. Startled, I pushed back and landed flat on my back in the yard. Quickly, I skittered against the grass and pressed my body firmly against the house as the dog began to howl and bark.

"Dog, what are you barking at?" the old man shouted as a beam of light cast out over the yard. Oh crap, someone had moved the curtains and was looking out the window. I gazed at Scooter, his eyes wide and his face white, like he had seen a ghost. We were both in disbelief, shocked, and we didn't want to get caught eavesdropping. I raised my finger to my lip to silence him. We remained still as the old man loomed over us. It felt like minutes, but I'm sure it was only seconds before the beam of light disappeared, the barking stopped, and the old man pulled the curtains shut and the dog away.

A sigh of relief flooded over me. I cautiously eased my way back up to the edge of the window. I looked down. Scooter looked fatigued. He was shaking his head, and I could tell he wanted to leave—and honestly, so did I.

But I had come to get answers, and I didn't have them yet. I needed to know more. I cast a meaningful look at Scooter. I think he caught my drift. We weren't going anywhere just yet.

"That should keep that hound from barking," I heard Old Man Smithers say as a door slammed from farther inside the house. *Great, he put the dog in another room. What a lucky break!* "What were you saying, Tom?"

"As I was saying, I told you that in confidence, so I have to know… Did you go up to the cave?"

"Why on earth would I go to the cave? I told you I didn't care. That's all in the past."

Blood rushed to my head. What was all in the past? These two had a secret, and I needed to know what it was. *Come on, come on, say it. Please say it!*

"Well, I had to ask for Johnny's sake. I guess I've taken enough of your time."

"I told you that boy was trouble. If you ask me, I think you are beginning to like him!"

"He's a good kid… he deserves to know."

"You keep your mouth shut, or I'll tell his parents about our little secret."

Things were silent before I heard a shuffle, followed by the sound of the front door opening. *Oh crap, he's leaving!*

"Run, run," I mouthed to Scooter through gritted teeth.

# FIVE

Scooter shot to his feet, and I followed as we sprinted across the yard, making our way toward the tree line some fifty yards away. I knew that if Tom made it to his car and started the engine, the headlights would cast a bright light over the field and expose us.

We darted, but Scooter quickly fell a few steps behind me. I could hear him asking me to wait, whimpering as I pulled away. I had to make the tree line; I couldn't let Tom know I was spying on him. Tom couldn't do anything to Scooter if he got caught, but I worked for Tom. I needed him to trust me if I ever wanted to have a chance to work the cash register and work with the gas customers.

I never looked back, and part of me felt guilty as I plunged into the tall grass. I was exhausted and hunched over and placed my hands on my knees. I huffed and puffed, trying to catch my breath. Scooter burst into the tall weeds and collapsed to the ground, exhausted. I lowered myself down and sat next to him. The roar of the engine came to life in the distance. We peeked out from the tall blades of grass that offered us protection from the open field as the lights flicked on. We both chuckled. We made it!

Tom backed up, turned the car around, and beelined down the driveway. The car vanished as we watched him turn onto Old Lizardville Road. Scooter and I were in the clear; we laughed and smiled as we rose. I grabbed my bike and started to push it toward the woods. We walked side by side down the mountain path, giving us the much-needed time to discuss what I had heard. I wanted to make sure I remembered the words correctly. Telling Scooter over and over engrained them in my head.

"Wait a minute," Zack exclaimed. "You talk about ghosts like they're real. And you snuck around in the middle of the night and spied on people. But you get upset when I come home a few minutes late from Larry's house?" He smiled, thinking he had me in a pickle.

"I'm talking about thirty years ago; times were different back then. We knew everyone. We lived in a small town with only a few hundred people. It was safe to be out at night," I explained to my boys.

"No, that doesn't fly," Daniel chimed. "Zack and I know the people in our neighborhood. We're safe here."

"I don't think you're as safe as you think you are. We live in the suburbs. Over a million people live here. Do you know them all?" I smirked.

Daniel and Zack exchanged a few looks. Finally, Zack admitted that they didn't know everyone. I must admit, I didn't know everyone in my hometown either, but that would be our little secret.

"Dad, you didn't know Tom and Old Man Smithers had a secret." He smiled, thinking he'd outsmarted me.

"You're right, but neither would have killed me!" I explained. I think the boys thought they had me backed into a corner, and quickly, I switched things back. "Do you want me to continue with my story or not?"

Zack and Daniel both nodded and settled back into their chairs. Outside, the wind howled, and the rain pelted the windows as the storm raged on. My mind darted to Sara, who had to be out on a night like this. Yes, I was concerned that she hadn't texted me to let me know she had returned to work. I looked at the boys and rubbed my hand across my chin. *Now, where was I?*

Scooter and I were walking our bikes back, discussing the events of the evening. After dropping him by his house, I peddled my bike the rest of the way home. Mother and Father were watching our new colored TV in the other room. I poked my head in the room to let them know I was home before I stomped up the stairs to my room.

Buck was spending the night at Parker's house, so I had the room to myself—what a relief. I grabbed the "A" encyclopedia, hoping to find something on the ax factory, and there were a few entries. Unfortunately, there was nothing on the one in Pennsylvania. Then I grabbed the book labeled "T," praying I would find something about the Thornhills—just another dead end, as I had feared.

"Why didn't you Google it?" Zack smirked.

"They didn't have Google back then, dummy!" Daniel responded.

"Daniel," I lashed out, "don't call your brother a dummy. We don't call anyone that. Do you understand?" I waited for his response.

He frowned. "Yes, sir."

"But I wish we had Google back in the 70s. Searching for information would have been much easier."

With my book research leading to a dead end, I grabbed *Moby Dick*, an old favorite of mine, from the bookshelf and started to read.

I woke up to the sun shining through my window and the book beside me on the bed. I guess I had fallen asleep. I couldn't believe it was morning already. But that was a good thing. I smiled, bounced out of bed, ran downstairs, showered, and dashed back to my room for clean clothes. My tummy growled as I made my way to the kitchen. Mom already had a bowl of Quisp cereal on the table. I added the milk and dug in. In no time, I was scraping the bottom of the bowl. Then slowly, I raised the bowl, tilted it to my lips, and drank every last drop of the Quisp-flavored milk. I pushed my chair away from the table, glided across the kitchen floor, laid the bowl in the sink, kissed my mom on the cheek, and told her I was off to Parker's house.

"Don't forget to push your chair in."

"Sorry." I stopped and pushed the chair under the table as she asked. Then I turned and headed to the door.

I plowed my way outside, the screen door slamming behind me, grabbed my bicycle, and spun it around. One, two, three steps… I tossed my leg over the bar, planted my butt firmly on the seat, and began peddling. The air was cool and crisp; I thought about returning to grab my jacket, but I didn't have time. I was anxious to get with the others and see if they had any news to share.

I started the mile-long trek to Parker's house. I wasn't far down the road when I heard squawking on my left side. I ducked my head just in time. Gosh, I didn't even see the crow sitting in the trees. How could I have missed that? He was such a large bird and came out of nowhere. The crow dive-bombed over and over again. Each time I ducked as he just missed me. I wasn't sure if he wanted to hurt me—I think it was more like a scare tactic, but why? The crow had to be the old man. What was his name again? *Donald Thornhill*. Was I getting close to solving the mystery? Did the ghost know this? Had the others been attacked too, or was it just me? My mind went into overdrive, and I peddled faster.

I ducked again, but I felt his claws latch onto my shoulder this time. I quickly jerked the bike to the right, trying to get him off, but I lost my balance and flew over the handlebars. I hit the gravel, sliding several feet, palms down in the dirt. The bike stopped next to me, the back wheel spinning. My face was covered in dust; I spit a few times, trying to get the dirt taste out of my mouth. My hands hurt and felt ripped open. I turned them over as the blood came to the surface of my palms.

I hadn't had an accident like this in several years. It made me think back to the days when I was learning how to ride a bike; I got bumps and bruises all the time. But this accident wasn't my fault. This was a vicious attack. I gained my composure, rolled over, and gave a meaningful look to the sky, spotting the crow just in time as he made another run at me. I grabbed my bike and jerked it on top of me as a shield from his sharp claws. He swooped down again and again but was not able to get past the spokes on the wheel. A little relief flooded over me as I watched him fly away.

*Would he try again?* The crow quickly turned and came back at me. Well, that answered my question. He wasn't done with me. Much to my surprise, he stopped mid-flight and pulled back, stretching out his wings. He bobbed up and down a few times, squealed loudly, and cawed at me. He was taunting me. I squirmed and looked around for my escape route. Wait, I realized he wasn't teasing or playing with me but defending himself. In all the confusion, I hadn't noticed Parker and Buck throwing rocks and running toward the bird. The cavalry had arrived. I'm glad our house was only a mile from Parker's.

I repeatedly yelled at the crow, my bravery rising every second as I watched him turn and fly toward the woods. Parker and Buck raced to my side.

"Dude, you alright?" Buck smiled, looking down at me as he lifted the bike off.

"I'm fine, just a few minor cuts and bruises." I was relieved the crow was gone. I'm sure he was watching the three of us somewhere in the trees. Parker helped me to my feet, and we started to walk.

"Dude, your mom's going to kill you," Parker snickered, pointing to the rip in my new Levi's jeans. My heart sank. Parker was right. She would be upset, and I hoped I wouldn't get grounded again.

Buck smiled, throwing his arm around my shoulder. "You'll live," he said as he clamped his arm around my head and rubbed my hair with the other hand. We slowly made our way down the road.

A minute later, we arrived, and Parker dropped my bike on the porch. Everything seemed okay except for a broken spoke on the back rim. I felt confident I'd be able to ride it home later.

Parker pushed the door open, and I saw Lexi and Sara sitting on the couch. "Hi," I said with a gentle wave.

Sara gave me this funny look. She stared at me like she was a vulture, and I was her prey. Finally, she spoke, "What happened to you?"

"I had a run-in with a crow." I frowned.

"The dude was getting his butt kicked by a crow. Good thing we showed up to save his little behind." Buck smiled, glancing at Lexi, then Sara, as he started to laugh.

"I don't think it's funny," Sara hissed, then nodded to her sister for approval.

"She's right." Lexi frowned at Buck, then cast a nasty look at her brother.

"Listen, you need to wash up and put some Merthiolate on those cuts," Lexi demanded.

"Ah, I don't think so… that crap burns; plus, it will turn my hands red."

"Don't be a baby." Sara smiled.

That was the first time Sara had smiled at me in weeks. I think she enjoyed seeing me squirm. "Alright, I'll wash and put the red crap on my hands." I entered the bathroom, placed the stopper in the sink, and turned on the water. I waited a few seconds to ensure the water was nice and hot, then slowly inched my hands in. The dirt and small pieces of gravel came off quickly. I lifted my hands to get a better look at the damage. It wasn't as bad as I thought—just a few minor cuts, nothing too deep. *I'm no doctor, but I guess I'll live*. After cleaning my hands, I grabbed the dark-colored washcloth, soaked it with water, and wrung out the excess. I bent down and pulled up my torn jeans to expose my knee. I began to wipe; I saw a few scratches but nothing serious. I rinsed the towel and wrung the cloth again, leaving the excess blood in the sink. I repeated the process over and over until my knee was clean.

My hands and knee felt much better after being cleaned. Now came the hard part—putting the red junk on the cuts to fight off infection. "Dang," I screamed as the first drop hit my hand. I was interrupted by a knock at the door. Do you need some help?" Lexi muttered through the keyhole.

"I'm fine!" I said through gritted teeth.

The door sprang open. Lexi shook her head and grabbed the small red eyedropper from my hand. The smell of the medicine burned my nose. I knew this was going to hurt; it always did. I wouldn't say I liked Merthiolate and didn't know anyone who did.

"Show me your palms," she barked. With her free hand, she grabbed mine and pulled it toward her. I gritted my teeth again as I watched her put a few drops on my palm.

"Ouch, ouch, ouch, it burns," I cried, trying not to let any tears seep from my eyes. I would never hear the end of it if I shed any tears. I puckered up my lips and began to blow on my palms. *Ah, that's a bit better.*

"Don't be a baby." Sara giggled from the doorway.

"I'm almost done," Lexi reminded me. "There, that should do it. How about your knee?

"The knee is fine, no scratches or cuts," I lied.

She smiled. "Okay… it's *your* knee."

"Thanks." I wasn't sure what else to say. The pain still lingered in my hands.

"We were about to head to the library to see if we could find out anything about Donald Thornhill. Do you wanna join us?" Lexi smiled.

"Sure." I returned the smile. I stood up and followed them into the living room, and then I brought everyone up to speed about what Tom and Old Man Smithers were talking about last night. Everyone agreed that something smelled fishy. Buck and Parker lagged behind. I guess it was because they didn't want to go to town—or should I say go to the library. They made excuses, saying they had other errands to run, so it would just be Lexi, Sara, and me.

# SIX

We left in a single file, with me bringing up the rear. I climbed into the back seat of Lexi's dad's 1970 light blue Chevy Impala station wagon—his pride and joy. He'd purchased the new car six years ago. It didn't have a scratch on it, and we intended to keep it that way. Lexi turned the key, and the engine roared to life. Lexi had been driving for a little over a year now. Part of me was scared to drive a car, but on the other hand, I couldn't wait until I was old enough to learn—it meant freedom.

Lexi put the car in reverse, and I listened to the gravel driveway crunch under the tires as she backed the car up. Placing the car into drive, we lurched forward and pulled the old station wagon out of the driveway and onto Old Lizardville Road. For a minute, I thought Lexi was going to Mill Hall, but I quickly realized she was heading to Lock Haven, which made sense since its library had the most extensive collection in the area. We passed through Mill Hall and proceeded toward Lock Haven, up one hill and down another. Several minutes later, Lexi pulled the car to the rear of the library. She parked at the back of the lot, ensuring no other vehicles were parked close to ours. I'm sure she remembered the last thing her dad yelled, "No scratches."

We sat for a minute, trying to decide how to handle this so as not to arouse suspicion. Lock Haven was still a small town, and news traveled fast. The last thing we needed was for someone to think we were looking for information about the Ax Factory Murders. I think we were acting a little paranoid, though.

Lexi swung her door open, and Sara and I did the same. I stepped out, placed my feet on the asphalt parking lot, and glanced right, then left—the coast looked clear. I took off quickly and made my way to the entrance. The girls hung back a little before dashing to the front door. We were trying to give the illusion that we were not together. How silly was that since no one else was around? They slowly made their way up the steps, and I opened the door for the girls—I hoped Sara would notice I was a gentleman. I entered behind the ladies and noticed that Lexi and Sara had stopped a few feet inside the entrance. They looked lost. I motioned my head toward the card files. We would start there to see what books they had about the Thornhills. I trekked over, quickly found the "T" section, pulled the long drawer out, and began thumbing through the card catalog. *Th, Tho, Thor, I was getting closer. Thorn's* "Oh, lookie here." I smiled as I pulled out a four-inch by six-inch index card.

I held it up as if I had found a lost treasure. "*The Thornhills of Pennsylvania*, by Laurence Daniels," I whispered to the girls. "I think this is what we're looking for." The card had a brief synopsis and contained information about where we would locate the book. It was in the history section, aisle two, section seven, shelf five. My emotions were running high. This was the moment I had been waiting for—this should answer all our questions, or at least I hoped it would. I pointed in the direction we needed to go, then glanced around the large room to ensure no one was watching us. I smiled to myself. *Guess I've read too many spy novels*. I followed Lexi and Sara to aisle two but turned my head one last time to make sure no one followed before I quickly entered the row.

One, two, four, six, ah… section seven. "Here it is," I whispered. I glanced up at shelf number five. There were many books on the shelf, and Lexi and I started looking for the book on opposite ends. We fingered our way toward the middle, glancing at each other as we neared the center. Sara stood a few feet away and remained silent. Lexi and I could tell something was wrong. The book was missing; this had to be a mistake. *Okay, please don't panic*, I thought to myself. Lexi moved down to the next shelf, and I started leafing through the books on the shelf below, but still no luck.

I thought it was peculiar that the book I needed had been checked out. Who else would want to read a book about the Thornhills? Glancing in sections six and eight, we still found nothing. Ten minutes passed, and I was tired and ready to give up when Lexi suggested we ask for help. We walked to the main desk, where the head librarian stood behind the counter.

"May I help you?" she asked, looking at all of us.

I felt a stiff shove in the middle of my back as Lexi pushed me forward. "Ah… Hi."

"Yes, may I help you?" she asked again.

"Yes, ma'am, I was looking for a book." The librarian stared at me, and her eyes drilled through me like laser beams. I don't know why I was having so much trouble getting the words out of my mouth.

"Can I help you find a book?" She seemed a little edgy as she spoke.

"Yes, I was looking for *The Thornhills of Pennsylvania*." I handed her the card to show her the exact book I wanted. She turned around, pulled open the drawer behind the counter, and leafed through the library cards to see if the book had been checked out.

"I'm sorry; that book's been checked out." She held a card in her hand. "Can I help you find anything else?"

"What do you mean *checked out*?" I grumbled.

"Someone else is reading the book, young man, and I resent your tone."

"I'm sorry, ma'am. I'm working on a history project for school, and I need this book to complete my report." I frowned.

She leaned over the counter. "Is there a period in time you were looking for?"

"Yes, something around the turn of the century. Ah, around 1904," I shyly said.

"We don't get many kids here investigating the Ax Factory Murders." She grinned. "I have some old newspaper articles that are on microfilm. You might find them helpful." She pointed at the microfiche machines. "Take a seat over there, and I'll bring them over in a minute."

I was baffled. "How did the librarian know what we were looking for?" I whispered, and Lexi and Sara shrugged. Something was off. I glanced around the room, then back to the counter. I watched as she disappeared into the back room. We walked toward the long table where three fancy new machines sat covered in plastic. I had never used one before, but from the looks of it, Lexi had. She removed the cover and pulled up a chair next to mine. She clicked the power button, and the screen turned white as the light came on.

"Here you go," the voice over my shoulder stated. I watched her lay a large stack of film sheets on the table. They looked odd to me—see-through paper sheets with small blocks of scribble embedded on them, each about the size of a postage stamp. Upon a closer look, I could see the headline from local newspapers. *How cool was that— a complete newspaper on a sheet of film paper?* Lexi grabbed the first sheet, slid it into the machine, and closed the tray.

The first sheet was dated December 3, 1953. She quickly pulled this one out and slid in another. One after another we continued; it could take all day at this rate. We were at it for over an hour when we came to the one that was dated June 11, 1904. The headline and photo caught our attention: "Ax Factory Owner Commits Suicide"—*The Lock Haven Express.*

*Local business owner, Donald Thornhill, was found dead in his home from an apparent self-inflicted gunshot wound to the head. Local officials found the body, but his wife, Annabelle Thornhill, is still missing. From the blood found at the scene, the police suspect foul play. The search continues in the hills behind the Thornhill residence. Police say the only survivor was the couple's three-year-old daughter, who was found hiding in the closet. She was taken to the local hospital and is still in shock and unable to provide any clues as to what happened the evening of June 9th.*

*Police are also looking for a missing man, Jacob Adams, a possible suspect in connection to the missing woman and suicide. He was reported missing the same evening and was an employee of the plant. Witnesses say Jacob and Annabelle were sweethearts when they were in high school.*

*The future of the ax factory comes into question as people wonder who will take ownership of the facility. According to sources close to the family, they were not having any financial issues.*

"Wow," I whispered. "Is there more?"

"No, that's it." Lexi frowned as she traced her fingers around the picture of Don Thornhill.

"How can that be it? There has to be more!" I urged.

"I think he has a funny mustache," Sara added.

Lexi, Sara, and I spent another twenty minutes searching through the old records. We checked every page and came up empty. My body trembled, sending goosebumps up my neck and down my arms. We went forward and back six weeks to ensure we didn't miss anything.

Something didn't feel right. "Do you hear that?" I glanced at Lexi and Sara as I raised a finger to my lips to silence them. We all paused, and our heads turned back and forth.

"I hear nothing," Sara whispered.

"Me neither," Lexi chimed.

"Exactly, it's too quiet," I said, "even for a library." You could hear a pin drop. Our chairs screeched on the floor as we pushed away from the table. The noise echoed off the walls. I glanced toward the main counter. Where was the librarian? I noticed the hands on the giant clock behind the counter had stopped moving. Was time standing still? And where was everybody? The place was empty. I was spooked and felt threatened, especially after this morning's attack on my bike.

We all took a step away from the table. Sara looked at me, and I could tell she was petrified. I wasn't sure what I could do to help her, but I stepped closer and whispered, "Everything's going to be fine. Just walk toward the door." I placed my arm around her shoulder, trying to reassure her. We huddled together as we inched closer to the front door. We glanced left, then right—the place was empty. It made no sense. Where had everyone gone? We pushed our way slowly toward the exit. Nervousness and panic raced through our veins.

Lexi put her hand on the handle to push. *What if the door is locked?* I exhaled a sigh of relief as I watched the door slowly glide open. Lexi planted her feet outside; Sara and I brought up the rear. I watched the door close, and we smiled at one another. Lexi began to giggle, as did Sara. A happy feeling flowed over us as we realized our minds must have been playing tricks on us.

Our confidence faded as I spotted the large crow perched on the power line across the street. *I've seen this bird before.* Our smiles and laughter disappeared, and I wondered why we parked so far from the door.

I had a notion that was not good, but it was the only thought that came to mind. "Give me the keys. I'll run to the car, unlock the doors, and drive here to pick you up," I said bravely.

"You don't know how to drive," Lexi retorted.

She was right. I didn't. I'd seen Lexi and my parents drive many times, and Buck was already learning to drive. I mean, how hard could it be?

"I'll tell you what. Take the keys," she said, placing them in the palm of my hand. "Run to the car, unlock the doors, and we'll be right behind you."

I could tell she was serious. My palms felt sweaty, the keys heavy in my hand. *Okay, you can do this,* I repeated in my head. "Are you ready?"

Lexi and Sara nodded. I briefly smiled at Sara with a slight nod to ensure she knew everything would be fine. I bounced on the balls of my feet—yes, I was horrified. Taking a deep breath, I plunged down the stairs and broke toward the car. Rapidly, I darted between the parked cars and sprinted across the wide-open space of the back lot. Just a few more steps and I would be home free. I skidded to a stop next to the car and fumbled when I tried to insert the key into the lock. "Ah, come on, come on, get in there," I whispered. I heard the crow caw as the key slid into the lock. I turned the key and listened for the click, then grabbed the handle as I opened the door. I lunged inside and slammed the door behind me. I felt safe, and I quickly unlocked the other front door, then plunged into the back and did the same on both sides of the car.

I looked out the window and spotted Sara and Lexi weaving in and out of the parked cars, and then they broke into the open part of the lot. My head spun around to look at the tree line and noticed the crow was still there. Then the oddest thing happened. I watched as the crow faded as if it had never been there. The driver's side car door flung open, and I screamed as the other side door flew open in the back. It was the girls getting in—nothing supernatural. My breathing slowed, and my heart returned to my chest. I pointed toward the far side of the lot, just below the trees. Lexi's mouth dropped open, as did Sara's.

"Where'd the crow go?" Lexi asked. I shrugged, not knowing the answer.

Suddenly, a ghostly white vapor emerged in front of the car. We sat in silence and watched. A man dressed in work clothes from the turn of the century appeared. He had a short beard and a funny-looking mustache. I rubbed my eyes; I couldn't believe what I saw. *This can't be real.*

"Do you see it?" My voice shook. The twisted look on Sara's and Lexi's faces answered my question. The old man smiled. His teeth looked dirty. Then he chuckled a bit. I could tell he was enjoying this.

"I've got my eyes on you three." He paused. "I can tell you're up to no good," he hissed and smiled, his rotten teeth showing. "You girls should be careful with the company you keep; that boy may get you killed." He pointed at me. *Wait . . . killed? Did I hear him right? I couldn't be sure since the windows were rolled up.* Sara ducked into the back seat and started to cry. I laid my hand on her shoulder. Lexi pushed back in the front seat, but there was nowhere to hide. Then, as quickly as he had changed from a crow to a man, he vanished into thin air.

We sat in disbelief for several minutes. Finally, Sara broke the silence when she whimpered, "Can we get out of here?"

Lexi brought the car to life with a turn of the key. Her hands trembled on the steering wheel as we slowly left the parking lot. The drive back to their house was extended, quiet, and uneventful. Thank goodness for small miracles.

# SEVEN

As we pulled into the driveway, I spotted Scooter and Todd chatting on the porch. The front door flew open, and out lunged Parker and Buck. Perfect, everyone was here. The minute the engine shut off, I jetted from the car, and the girls were right on my heels. "Everyone, upstairs!" Lexi waved her hand in a circular motion as if she were rustling cattle into a corral. "Upstairs, now," she barked again. "I'm talking to all of you."

I followed the others through the front door. Mr. and Mrs. Parker were dressed in nice clothes and about to leave. Lexi tossed her dad the keys, thanked him, and continued to the attic. Mrs. Parker's stare burned the back of my head as I walked by. One minute she was excited that I was taking Sara to the dance, the next, she was mad at me—all because someone assumed Sara and I were up to no good.

One by one, we marched upstairs, past Lexi's bedroom and then Sara's, and we continued to the end of the hall. Lexi looked over her shoulder to make sure we were all there before opening the attic door. It made a loud creaking sound as it swung open, and with the flick of a switch, the lights lit up the stairwell, and I watched her climb out of sight.

As I began climbing, I heard Todd say, "What's up with you guys and attics? Can't we talk downstairs?" Parker and Buck laughed. I smiled as I took my spot on the attic floor between Sara and Scooter. I watched the others take their places in the circle.

"What's so urgent?" Parker asked, gazing at his sister.

Lexi peered out the far side attic window to see if their parents had left, then turned to face the group. "As you know, we went to the library. We found out that the legends are not like the story goes. You see, they never found Annabelle's body." Parker, Todd, and Buck looked baffled. "Then the old man showed up in the parking lot—"

"What old man?" Buck interrupted.

"The ghost of Donald Thornhill," she blurted out, and the room fell silent.

"What'd he want?" Parker questioned, breaking the silence.

"He warned us to back off. That's all. But we're fine, so let me continue," Lexi urged. "Here's what we know. We found this old newspaper article that said the old man committed suicide, and they found his body in the home. But they never found Annabelle or Jacob." Lexi paused and took a deep breath. "So, what happened to her body? Did he bury her before he took his life?"

"He had to." The words flew out of my mouth before I realized.

She pointed to me excitedly. "My thoughts exactly, but why?"

"That's easy… he loved her," Sara added in a sheepish voice. I was impressed that she was participating.

"We could ask Annabelle where her remains are," Scooter added.

"I doubt she's gonna tell us," Todd advised.

"You're probably right, but something isn't adding up." I shrugged. "We know some of the facts but not enough. They found the old man's body but never Jacob's or Annabelle's. We know where he buried Jacob, and we might be able to ask Annabelle about her remains. But how does this tie back to Tom Evans or Old Man Smithers? Then there's Jimmy. Does he know something to help us return these ghosts to the other side?"

"Good points, all of them." Lexi smiled.

"Maybe the answers are in the book," Sara said. Wow, Sara was two for two on stating the facts.

"What book?" Buck asked.

"Maybe they are… We need to get our hands on that book and see what secrets it holds. In the meantime, we need to talk to Jimmy and Annabelle," Lexi demanded.

"What book?" Buck asked again.

"It takes every piece to complete a puzzle," I said. "I'll work on getting the book from the library, and you two work on getting answers from Jimmy and Annabelle."

"What book?" Buck snapped.

"The Thornhill book at the library, but it was checked out, so I'll have to go back." I beamed at Buck.

"Thank you."

"Why not request their presence now so we can ask them?" the soft voice said, steady and slow. Wow, Sara was three for three. We all looked at each other. I could tell they had the same question: How do we get them to show up? Do we have to do a séance?

"Do you have encyclopedias?" I asked.

"Sure," Lexi nodded.

I jumped up, and Lexi followed. "We'll be right back," she called. I heard the others chatting as we bolted down the stairs. Lexi went ahead of me to their family living room and pointed toward the bookshelves on the far wall. I was compelled to find out the answer and solve this mystery.

*Ah, a nice set of Britannia encyclopedias.* I scrolled my finger from left to right, looking for the book labeled "S," and there it was. Using my index finger, I tilted the book's top toward me before wrapping my hand around it.

"Make sure there's a chapter about how to conduct a séance," Lexi said.

"Great idea." I didn't want to go back upstairs with it only to find nothing to explain the process.

"Whatcha doing?" A deep voice resonated behind us. Startled, I jumped and lost my grip on the book, which sent it toppling to the floor. A wave of chills raced up my spine.

Lexi was startled too. She must have jumped a foot off the ground when she heard his voice. "Hey, Dad, you scared us. Um... I thought you left?"

"We did, but your mother forgot this," he said, waving a small handbag before us. "We're leaving now. Have a good evening."

"Okay, have fun." Lexi smiled.

"We'll be back in a little while, and keep an eye on your sister and this one," he said before he turned to the door.

"I will, Dad. Love you," she called to him.

"Don't overdo it," I whispered. We watched Lexi's dad close the door behind him. I bent over and picked up the book. Lexi and I gazed at each other and chuckled a bit. The moment was already tense, and we didn't need any more interruptions.

I opened the book and raced with my fingers to find *séance*. *SC, SD, ah, SE…* my heart was pounding. I was getting close. I could feel it. There it was, *how to conduct a séance*. I started to read out loud.

*A séance is an event in which the living try to get in touch with someone from the spirit world. Typically, a group gathers to create a welcoming atmosphere and invite the spirit or spirits to answer questions or deliver a message to someone who passed away. The most important rule for conducting a séance is that everyone present must believe it is possible to talk with the other side. While communicating with spirits can be frightening, since we tend to fear what we cannot fully understand, the following steps will guide you in having a successful séance.*

> *Step 1. Light three candles and place them in the middle of a round table.*

> *Step 2. Sit in a circle around the table and hold hands; you do not want to break the ring once the séance begins.*

> *Step 3. One person must act as a medium.*

> *Step 4. You must have three or more participants.*

> *Step 5. Dim or turn off the lights.*

*Step 6. Everyone must chant in unison; the exact words, you may choose yourself. An experienced medium will instruct you to follow their lead.*

*Did you know the word séance comes from the French and means to sit or assemble?*

"Interesting," I whispered to myself. My imagination was running wild, and I couldn't help but notice Lexi was beaming excitedly too.

"Wait one minute," Daniel blurted out, cutting me off. "You all held a séance? Did it work? Who showed up? Were you scared?" He fired so many questions at me in a matter of seconds that my head began to spin.

"Hey, goofball, let him finish, and he'll answer all your questions," Zack told his younger brother.

"Now, now, no need for name-calling. Your brother's excited, and they say there is no such thing as a stupid question. These are all great questions." I turned to Daniel. "But Zack's correct, too. I will answer all of these questions when I continue my story."

"See," Zack retorted, and Daniel stuck out his tongue.

I shook my head at the boys and smiled.

"Why didn't you use Google? Or look it up on YouTube?" Daniel asked.

"You're not very smart, are you? Stupid head," Zack blurted out again.

"Hey, what did I say about the name calling," I snarled and shook my finger at Zack. Then I turned toward Daniel and spoke in a softer voice. "You must remember, it was the seventies, and the Internet wasn't born yet. We didn't have smartphones, Google, or YouTube. The library and encyclopedias were all we had and the best way to learn about people, places, and things, which is why I love books. We learn from them. Even if it's just fiction, we still learn something."

A sense of pride came over me. The boys were enjoying my story, and I loved this time with them. The power was still out, so I lit another candle and set it on the end table to add more light to the room. I rechecked my phone to see if Sara had texted me, but still nothing. I frowned. The storm was beginning to subside, yet off in the distance, you could still hear the roar of thunder.

Lexi and I were eager to get started and dashed to the kitchen. One by one, she opened and closed the drawers. Finally, she paused, pulled three candles out, and handed them to me. I found it hard to balance the load when it dawned on me that I was still holding the large book. Next, she darted to the other side of the room, grabbed a pack of matches, and tossed them at me. I barely made the catch.

"I think that's it." She smiled and started toward the stairs. Like a good boy, I followed, carrying everything while her arms remained empty. We pounded our way back upstairs. I could hear the others chatting. Todd, Parker, and even Buck doubted we could summon Annabelle or Jimmy to the attic. Even though Jimmy was our friend and we were doing this for him, I also had doubts, but we had to try.

Lexi hurried down the stairs and flicked the lights off before returning to the attic. One spot remained, and I took my seat next to Sara. I caught a glimpse of a smile on her face. My knees felt weak, and my stomach quickly turned to knots. A feeling rushed over me, one I had never felt before. I was about to hold Sara's hand, something I had only done once before but never for this long. I could feel the goosebumps rise on my arms. I wondered how she would feel.

"Okay, I need everyone to move a little bit and form a circle," Lexi requested. We all shuffled, trying to form the perfect circle for Lexi. She leaned forward and placed the three candles in the middle. I tossed the matches to her. Pulling a match from the pack, she struck it across the rough surface, and I watched as the bright yellow flame roared to life. Slowly, she moved it from one candle to the next, and we watched as the light of the flames flickered around the room.

"I'll do the talking," Lexi said, and we all nodded. "Let's all join hands and be as quiet as possible." The moment of truth arrived, and I interlocked my fingers with Sara. Her hand felt warm and a bit sweaty. I'm sure mine felt the same. Her facial expression never changed. Maybe it was only me who had this weird feeling inside.

"Next, I need you all to turn your attention to Jimmy and Annabelle. I know we all believe in ghosts because we've seen them." She paused and took a deep breath. The room was dark; only the candlelight dancing on the walls enabled us to see. My enthusiasm spiked, and from the look on everyone's faces, we all felt the same.

"Annabelle Thornhill and Jimmy Brooker, we request your presence today in this attic. Please make yourself known to us," Lexi whispered slowly and repeated this several times. "We know you're out there, so please show yourselves, Annabelle Thornhill and Jimmy Brooker. Come forward and show yourselves. We know you can hear us." She repeated this several more times to no avail. Five, maybe ten minutes had passed, and still nothing from Jimmy or Annabelle, only the sound of candle wax dripping to the floor and Lexi's voice echoing off the walls.

"What a joke," Parker yelled and leaped to his feet, breaking the circle. He strode toward the stairs and turned. "Don't you see they're not coming?" He shook his head and pounded down the stairs.

"We don't need him," I threw out. "Plenty of us are left, but we must believe before they will come." I nodded my head, trying to reassure everyone. Lexi, Sara, and Scooter seemed to agree, but I wasn't sure about Buck or Todd. I stared at them. "Well," I looked directly at them, "are you in or out?"

Buck turned to face Todd as Todd gazed back. I wondered if they were ever going to speak to each other. I watched the moments tick away. Then finally, a few words slipped from Todd's mouth. "I'd like to see if this works."

"Me too," Buck agreed, taking Todd's hand, and the rest of us joined hands so we could continue.

# EIGHT

The six of us tightened our circle. I closed my eyes when Lexi began to chant, her words soft as they rolled off her tongue. "Annabelle Thornhill and Jimmy Brooker, we summon you here to this attic. Come forth and make your presence known." The minutes passed, and I was beginning to doubt anyone would show. Then I felt a light breeze. A chill ran up my spine; the hair on the nape of my neck stood. A wave of cool air rushed through the room. *Something was happening.* I opened my eyes and noticed Sara, Lexi, and Todd had done the same. The wind increased, and I shivered as the cold air flowed over me.

A weary voice moaned. I couldn't make out the words. I looked left, then right. It appeared to have come from the corner of the room. Lexi continued to whisper, "Annabelle Thornhill and Jimmy Brooker, we summon you here to this attic. Come forth and make your presence known."

The wind increased as the temperature continued to drop. Sara looked jittery, as did Scooter. Buck's and Todd's eyes darted around the room. I think we all felt anxious and excited at the same time. I had so many questions that only Jimmy or Annabelle could answer if I had a minute.

A twinkle of light emerged in the corner of the attic. It flickered, some sparks flew, and another blinked as the light grew. Our eyes remained fixed in that direction. My mind was ready to scream with excitement. I could barely contain myself as a mysterious image manifested in the corner. Seeing a ghost never gets old—it's unnatural, mysterious, and unexplainable. In one glorious moment, we witnessed an apparition make its presence known. Inside, I hoped it would be Jimmy—I felt safe around him. The image moved. The glowing orb of light grew brighter and slowly began to take shape. Lexi quickened her pace as the chanting continued. A shooting pain throbbed in my right hand, and my eyes darted downward to discover Sara squeezing my hand.

"You're safe… everything's fine," I comforted her. Our eyes met, and the pain relaxed in my fingers. I noticed a soft smile on her face before I turned my attention back to the corner.

Lexi had the momentum, and she continued to ramble. I bit my lip; the wait was killing me. There was another blinding flash, and I scrunched my eyes and blinked a few times to remove the spots floating across my vision. The glow took shape, and the lights subsided as Jimmy appeared. His body hovered—a transparent blue hue before us—but it was him. He was still wearing those corduroy shorts and sneakers from the day he drowned.

He frowned and appeared lost. I'd never seen this expression on his face before. His head moved from side to side. His eyes glazed over. I watched his lips part as if he were trying to say something, but I could barely make out the words. "Stop," his speech slurred, "you don't want to do this."

Lexi continued to chant though her voice was a bit muffled, and everything around me began to fade. It felt like Jimmy and I were the only ones in the room. "We need your help. Can you help us?"

"This isn't a good idea," he repeated. "Annabelle hates this house… Don't you remember? She shared this house with Donald, and this is where Jacob was murdered, her one true love." His strength appeared to fade.

"I'll be quick, Jimmy. Can you answer some questions?"

He frowned. "Be quick."

I noticed the others look at me, then back to Jimmy. *Was I the only one with questions? Or were they all too scared to ask?* "Why is Donald Thornhill after me?"

Jimmy stared at me for a moment. "If you've seen him, that's not good." He looked at the floor. "You're messing with things you shouldn't." He paused. "It's about revenge. Annabelle loved Jacob, not Donald. She only loved his money, nothing more, so he seeks revenge because he thinks you're helping her."

"Can Donald hurt us? Or kill us?" I guess I never thought about it like that.

"Of course… Annabelle killed me." Jimmy frowned. "Even though it was an accident, she succeeded."

Jimmy made a good point. The day he drowned. That day on the water, Annabelle leaped into his body and forced him over the dam.

"Donald could step into your body and take control. He's that powerful. He even has the ability to move and throw objects, even transform them into anything he likes.

It would be best to be careful around him. He's dangerous," Jimmy warned.

"I've seen him a few times. He knocked me off my bike and visited me at the library. I'm nervous, Jimmy," I hinted.

He grimaced. "That's not good."

"How can we stop him?" I asked.

Jimmy hovered close to me. "I'm not sure. Maybe Annabelle would know." He closed the gap between us in a split second. He floated inches from my face before darting away and circling the attic. He paused to glance at each of us. Sara smiled, and he returned her smile. Scooter, Todd, and Buck smiled, too. "Where's Parker?"

I shrugged. "He's downstairs." In a flash, Jimmy vanished. Never breaking stride, Lexi continued to chant. A loud noise erupted downstairs—screams and a thud—and moments later, I heard footsteps pounding on the stairs. The door flew open, and Parker stumbled in with a smiling Jimmy behind him. Parker remained silent as he sat on the floor next to Todd.

Jimmy giggled. "Now we're all here." By the smile on his face, I could tell he enjoyed tormenting Parker. He did when he was alive, so why would that change because he was a ghost?

"If we can't stop Donald or Annabelle," I frowned, "then how can we help you?"

"We could help him cross over," Scooter suggested. My eyes darted toward Jimmy.

I didn't want Jimmy to leave. After all, he was still my friend. But I wanted his soul to be at peace.

The temperature dropped again. I wished I had brought a jacket with me. The wind whirled harder, and I watched Jimmy cower. Something or someone was coming, and I hoped it was Annabelle. "I warned you," Jimmy protested and backed away to the edge of the room.

Dust kicked up from the attic floor. The cold wind whirled around the room. A brilliant flash of light made us all blink, and Annabelle suddenly appeared in the circle before us. "How dare you summon me to this place?" she hissed.

I could see in her eyes that she was appalled. She mumbled a few words, raised her hands above her head, and moved them in a circular motion. The wind increased, and the cold air slapped me in the face. Sara put her hands over her head and lowered her body to the floor for protection, and Scooter followed.

"Stop it!" I barked.

She moved faster than light, her face only inches from mine. "How dare you speak to me?" she hissed.

"Annabelle, it's me, Johnny, Tom's friend. You remember your great-grandson, Tom, right?" The words stuttered out of my mouth. She briefly paused, then flung her hands out to her sides, and the wind ceased.

Dust and debris dropped and settled to the floor, the chill still in the room. But the wind tunnel was gone, for now at least.

Her eyes looked like fire, and I could tell she was furious. "I hate this house. Nothing but bad memories!" she yelled. "Why have you brought me here?" Her voice was slow and demanding.

"How do we stop Donald?" I got right to the point. I didn't know how long she would stay, and I didn't want to waste a second.

She paused to reflect. I could tell she was intrigued by the idea.

"How do we get rid of Donald?" I asked again in a weary voice.

"I would need to drag him to the underworld," she whispered.

"What?" I asked, my mouth agape. "What did you say?"

"I would need to drag him to the underworld," she repeated in a clear voice.

I was puzzled and taken aback by her comment. "But … I thought that was only something in a book."

"What?" She looked baffled. "You sit here in the presence of ghosts, and you think the underworld doesn't exist?"

"You're right." She had a valid point. I felt embarrassed to have even mentioned it. "So, how do you drag Donald to the underworld? Can we help?" The others looked at me like I was crazy, and maybe I was, but I just wanted all this to end.

She sighed. "It's something only I can do, but I won't."

My nose twitched and felt itchy; my lips felt chapped. A pungent smell filled the air. I scrunched my nose, trying to block the aroma. I looked at the others and could tell they smelled it, too. *Where was the odor coming from?* They knew what would happen from the looks on Jimmy's and Annabelle's faces. The rotten smell grew more robust, and I was about to throw up when a bursting display of fire and smoke erupted and climaxed with a loud boom. "Get out of my house," the tall man bellowed. "Get out of my house now!"

Jimmy slid back to the corner while the rest of us sat with our mouths agape. Lexi stopped chanting and only stared. Annabelle puffed herself up. "You're not welcome here, Donald," she snarled. "Get out! Get out!" Oh, she was building up steam and was about to blow.

Donald sneered at her. He seemed to be enjoying this. I was petrified and glanced at Sara and noticed the tears trickling down her trembling face. I held her hand tightly and tried to reassure her that we were safe. I noticed Scooter was whimpering on the floor, too. Buck jumped to his feet in protest, but before he could say anything, Donald waved his hand, and Buck fell to the floor like someone had pulled the rug right out from under his feet. Parker lunged up but barely got to his knees before crumpling to the floor. Donald was showing us exactly how powerful and in command he could be.

An abnormal feeling flowed over me like cold water rushing over a waterfall, yet I was dry. I began to stand, but I wasn't moving forward. I cocked an eyebrow. I had no control over my body—someone was controlling me, and I knew it had to be Donald. Panic crept in, and I tried to scuttle away. The momentum carried me toward Donald, and I stopped inches from his face. The air oozed out of my lungs, almost like I had been sucker punched. My eyes felt heavy, and I worried I would pass out. I noticed a beam of light, and a chill raced through me when I collapsed to the floor.

"Johnny… Johnny…" My eyes blinked, then slowly opened to the touch of Lexi's hand rubbing my face. I blinked again and spotted Lexi and Sara kneeling over me.

"What happened?"

"Jimmy saved you," Sara sobbed.

"What? How did I get here?" I repeated.

"Donald was pulling you in, controlling you somehow. You slowly glided across the room, and it looked like he was about to merge into your body when Jimmy beamed himself through you and straight into Donald. That led to an enormous explosion of light, and they both vanished."

I leaned forward, and my eyes darted around the room—the ghosts were gone.

Lexi chuckled. "It was amazing. How do you feel? Can you tell us how it felt?" she marveled.

"Let him be," Sara chided. "He's suffered enough."

I felt dizzy and nauseous. I sat there for a moment and noticed that the others were pleased I was awake. Buck, Parker, and Todd were making their way to the stairs, and I rubbed my head as they passed. Scooter smiled at me and extended a hand to help me to my feet. Sara stood beside me to help me balance. We made our way downstairs and gathered around the family living room. An hour later, I felt better and headed home, though I leaned on Buck most of the way. We marched upstairs, and Buck even tucked me into bed. I wasn't sure if this was brotherly love or the fact that he didn't want Father getting upset over my being sick.

I tried to recall the day's events as I lay in bed. I wondered if Jimmy was okay. He saved my life, or at least, I think he did. I still needed answers, but another puzzle piece had come together.

# NINE

I rolled out of bed. I hadn't felt this good in weeks. It's amazing what a good night's sleep will do for you. The events of yesterday loomed large in my mind. I felt sharp like all my senses had awakened. Could that be a side effect of Jimmy passing through me? Plus, I had some of the answers I needed. But there were still too many unanswered questions. What was Tom's role in all of this? And how did Old Man Smithers fit into the puzzle? And one of the biggest questions—who removed Jacob's remains? And why would they remove them, and where did they take them? Then it dawned on me—today was a school day, and I had better get ready, or I'd be late.

Like any other day, I went downstairs, had breakfast, and got myself ready for school. Buck and I waited next to the road until the bus came to a squealing stop. I sat next to Scooter, but my mind drifted to what Annabelle had said about taking Donald to the underworld. The bus stopped again, and Scooter nudged me to let me know we had arrived.

I hooked up again with Scooter during the second period and later at lunch. We didn't say much to each other—I guess he could tell my mind was preoccupied. I spent the rest of the day thinking about what questions I would ask Tom. Finally, the bell rang, and school was out for the day.

The squealing brakes stopped as I leaped from the bus stairwell and bolted toward the house. I bounced back down the stairs, my feet hitting every other step. I ran upstairs and quickly changed out of my school clothes.

"Slow down, mister," Mother yelled from the kitchen. "Where are you off to?"

"I have to be at work; I'll grab something to eat there if that's okay?"

"Hmm… sure, when will you be home?"

"I get off at eight, so shortly after that."

"Don't forget your homework," Mother said, and those were the last words I heard as I let the door close behind me. I grabbed my bike and peddled as fast as possible. Moments later, I was laying one of my famous skid marks with my rear tire next to the building as I jammed on the brakes and tossed my bicycle to the rear of the store.

I hopped around the front and threw the door open to hear the bells ringing overhead. *Great*, the place was empty. "Tom," I hollered.

"Back here."

I strode toward his office and shoved the door open. "Tom, we had a séance last night, and Jimmy and Annabelle showed up," I hollered. My mouth hung wide open, and Tom looked stunned. Across from him sat Old Man Smithers.

"Hello, Johnny." He smiled. "What was that you were saying?"

*What's he doing here? Why didn't Tom warn me?* I paused, thinking up an excuse. "I was talking about this movie I watched last night. They held a séance, and the ghost showed up." I lied.

"I thought I heard you say, 'Jimmy and Annabelle'?"

*What did he know about Jimmy and Annabelle?* I felt like a mouse in a room with a cat blocking the only way out. He had me cornered, and I didn't know how to respond. My stomach twisted, and I fretted about sharing anything with him. I stared at the old man, my mind blank. *Think*, I willed myself, *think*. I gazed at Tom.

Tom pushed his chair back and stood. He extended his hand to Mr. Smithers. "Thank you for stopping by. It's always great to catch up." Puzzled, the old man slowly pushed his chair back and rose to his feet, never breaking eye contact with me. We both knew Tom had saved the day. A heavy feeling came over me—I knew the old man wouldn't let this go. This was only the beginning.

I watched Tom walk him to the front door and around the other side of the building. I never thought to see if a car was parked on that side. I felt foolish and knew right away I had to be more careful.

The bells clanged, and Tom entered the office, analyzing me momentarily.

"For Christ's sake, what were you thinking? Coming in here and shouting about ghosts! Bob will have plenty of questions, and I had better come up with good answers." Tom frowned.

"I'm sorry, I didn't know—"

"Take out the trash and sweep the floors," he snarled.

I didn't say another word. I sidled past Tom and out the office door; I gathered garbage as I went about the store. When the bag was full, I made my way to the rear of the building, threw open the back door, and placed the bag on the burn pile. The cawing of a large crow startled me. My heart stopped. One awful moment after another, could this evening get any worse? The crow swooped down and landed before me as I raised my hands to protect my face. The bright light left me paralyzed. I winced, and Jimmy appeared before me. "Phew." I sighed as relief flooded over me.

"We need to talk, but not here. What time do you get off work?"

"E-Eight," I stuttered.

"Great, I'll be in your room." I could hear a desperate edge to his voice.

A smile cracked my face as I watched Jimmy evaporate. I was puzzled and couldn't wait to find out what he wanted. I quickly returned to work, saying very little to Tom until the end of my shift. It was ten minutes before eight when Tom called me to his office.

"Thanks for your help this evening. I greatly appreciate everything you do around here."

"No problem… Thanks for letting me work when my homework allows."

"School work comes first, I say, but I haven't seen you in a few days. I was beginning to wonder—"

"Sorry, I should have called; I've had so much homework lately, and I haven't felt the greatest, to be honest." I knew I was stretching the truth—okay, so I was lying—but I didn't feel great after the experience in the attic, and that should count for something.

"Glad you're feeling better. Oh, next time, make sure we're alone before you run your mouth," Tom said with a wry smile.

"I will," I smirked. I knew I had dodged a bullet. "Hey, Tom, can I ask you a question?"

He stopped writing in the ledger and looked up. "Sure, what's on your mind?"

I swallowed hard. "I was wondering what Old Man Smithers has to do with all of this?" Just like me, right to the point. I could tell I caught him off guard.

"I'm not sure I follow."

"Did he have anything to do with taking Jacob's remains?" Dang, two for two on the direct questions.

"I'm not sure." Tom took a deep breath. "How would he know about the body?"

"I was hoping you could tell me?" The question came out harsher than I expected.

After several minutes of dodging my questions, I felt I was wasting my time, so I threw in the towel. I said goodbye, grabbed my bike, and peddled as fast as I could toward the house. Jimmy would be waiting for me when I got home, and I was anxious to hear what he had to say.

My eyes darted from tree to tree. I expected an ambush. I stayed on the main road, assuming it would be safer. I peddled up our driveway, jumped off my bike, walked it up to the porch, and laid it down like I had done a thousand times. I wrapped my hand around the doorknob and slowly twisted it to the right, trying to make as little sound as possible. But of course, my mother hears everything. "Are you hungry?" she asked from the family room.

"No, I'm fine."

"Do you have homework?"

"Yes, I'll be in my room studying," I answered, going up the stairs. To my surprise, when I entered the room, it was empty. *Great, maybe Buck is working late.* That should give Jimmy and me plenty of time to talk.

A bright light illuminated in front of the attic door, and I immediately knew it was Jimmy. He appeared standing before me. I watched as he motioned me to the attic. He turned and passed through the door with ease. *That was so cool*, I thought. *I wish I could walk through walls.* I opened the door and quietly made my way up the squeaking steps.

Once I cleared the top step, I reached around until I found the pull string and yanked, turning on the light. I didn't need the light because Jimmy was putting off quite a glow, but I never knew when he would vanish, so I played it safe.

"Hi," I said.

"You're in danger, Johnny. Donald wants you to stop, and he'll do whatever it takes to make sure that happens," Jimmy spat out.

"I-I only want to help… we all do."

"What are you trying to accomplish?"

I paused. "We want you to be happy, and Annabelle too."

"That's never going to happen unless…" He paused and looked around. He sniffed the air like a dog trying to follow a scent, but I couldn't smell anything.

"What do you mean, *unless*? Tell me what we need to do." Jimmy had this awkward look on his face, a look I hadn't seen before. Something heavy was weighing on his shoulders.

"The only way…" he choked out, "the only way is to send him to the underworld, and we would need Annabelle to cross over to do that, which would require her cooperation."

"Okay, that's what she said the other night," I said, a little confused.

He looked me in the eye. "Once they're gone, you must help me cross over."

"Why?" I didn't want to see Jimmy go. "I mean, no. You can't leave."

"I don't belong here. At first, it was cool being a ghost. But it's been a year since the accident, maybe a little longer. Time stands still for me. I always watch you guys—enjoying life, playing, working, and eating. You know, I'll never taste food again." A tear traced a path down his cheek. "It's lonely on this side, not to mention that I'll be stuck here forever." I could tell he was hurting.

"But then I'll never see you again." I knew it sounded selfish when the words slipped from my tongue, and I watched Jimmy frown.

"Johnny, I love you like a brother, but I don't belong here," he said as his eyes welled up.

"How do I help you?" It hurt to say the words.

"Easy. Find my body and lay it to rest."

"Your body was never found."

He smirked. "I know where it is. I still go there from time to time."

I grappled with what he was asking me to do. "I can't go in the water and find your body," I gasped. "I just can't."

"I'm not asking you to. I can show you from the bank and tell you the location so you can show the divers." He gave me a half grin. "But first, we must take care of Donald Thornhill; then, you can help me."

"Sure," I was curious as to how we would send Donald to the underworld. So, what's our next move?"

"Let me talk to Annabelle. I'll see what I can learn." He extended his hand to shake mine, and without thinking, I reached for it and watched my hand pass through it. "Gotcha." He smiled, and I watched him fade before my eyes.

# TEN

The week passed with no new developments. School and work and Lexi's work schedule made it difficult to get to the library. I was beginning to wonder if we would get to the bottom of all this. I remained optimistic, though. Today was a new day. I picked up the phone and called Sara, and she gave me great news—Lexi was available. I called Scooter, who dropped by just in time to catch a ride with us to town. Now, if only the book I wanted was available, this would turn out to be a great day.

As we pulled into the library parking lot, I noticed I wasn't the only person looking around. Sara and Scooter both peered out the side window. I didn't see anything out of the ordinary, but that didn't mean someone—*or something*—wasn't lurking out of eyesight.

Lexi found a space in the front row next to the entrance. I guess she wouldn't take any chances with ghosts this time. The four of us bounced out of the car and up the steps. I held the door for the ladies, and I received little smiles from

Sara and Lexi. Sometimes it's the little things we do that can make others happy.

The girls, with Scooter at their side, went straight for the library catalog file cabinets. I knew they were searching for a book on how to help someone cross over to the other side. I went to see the librarian at the front desk.

"Hi, excuse me, ma'am." I smiled, trying to look over the large counter.

She leaned forward and returned my smile. "May I help you?"

I don't know why I felt so skittish. The librarian's eyes grew wide while she waited for me to answer. "Yes, I was here a week ago. Ah… there was this book that I wanted. *The Thornhills of Pennsylvania* by Laurence Daniels."

"Let me see what we have." She turned her back to me and started to rummage behind the counter. "Name?"

"Excuse me?"

Still facing the bookshelf, she turned her head toward me so I could hear her. "Your name, please?"

"Oh, it's Johnny."

She frowned. "Does Johnny have a last name?" Her tone sounded irritated.

"I'm sorry… Johnny Malone," I said. I had this bad habit of only giving half the story or half an answer. I knew improving my communication skills was something I needed to work on. Maybe it was just my age. After all, I was only fourteen.

I smiled as she turned to face me and laid the book on the counter. "School project?"

I nodded. "Yes."

"Just the one book?"

"Oh, ah… no, I wanted to look for another book." I turned and pointed toward the cabinets. "My friends are searching now."

"I'll keep this book here until you're ready to check out." She spun and tossed the book onto the back counter. She seemed annoyed with me, though I'm not sure why. I strode across the room and snuck up behind Sara and Scooter. Looking over Lexi's shoulder, I watched her thumb through the index cards.

"Any luck?" I barked in Sara's ear.

"Oh, you butthead." Sara jumped and rolled her eyes at me. Scooter was startled, too.

"Yes, I found two books." Lexi handed me both cards. *How to Release a Trapped Spirit* by Gerald Dupickle and *Defeating Dark Entities* by Gerald Dupickle. *Two books by the same author. This guy must be an expert on the spirit world.*

"These sound perfect, and they have the Thornhill book we need too," I added.

I read the cards and made my way toward aisle eight. I was surprised by how large the paranormal section was. I never realized so many people wrote about ghosts and supernatural stuff. It didn't take long, and we found both books. "I think that's it." I glided in stealth mode to the counter, feeling triumphant. Scooter was beside me while Lexi and Sara waited by the front door. I laid the books on the counter, and the librarian fumbled with the first card and furrowed her brow as she added today's date. She then repeated the process on the other books.

"Be careful, Johnny Malone… spirits are nothing to play with," she warned quietly before she turned and walked to her office.

My mouth hung open. *Was that a warning? Why would she care what I read?* I dismissed the warning; after all, I've seen ghosts and talked to them. I faced Scooter, and we walked over to join the girls. The minute we were in the car, I leafed through a few pages but found nothing interesting.

It had been a few days since I had checked the books out of the library, and time seemed to slip away. Between school, homework, and working at the store, I couldn't find the time to read the books. Why do teachers have to give so much homework? I also wondered why Lexi and Sara hadn't offered to help. I guess they only wanted the answers. And I knew Scooter wasn't about to read a book unless it was for a school project.

Finally, the weekend arrived, and I had minimal homework with only one assignment and the entire weekend ahead of me. Tonight would be the perfect time to dig into these books—and the hardest decision I faced was which book to read first.

After some debate, I chose *How to Release a Trapped Spirit*. The book started with most of the basics—how to have a séance and prepare. I already knew all of that. After several chapters, I decided I was wasting my time. I tossed that aside and picked up *Defeating Dark Entities*. Now, this was more my style. The more I read, the more I liked it. I was hooked. I turned another page and found some interesting facts.

*We have the ability to assist spirits who wish to move forward or cross over into the spiritual realm. When friends, loved ones, pets, or family members pass away, they* generally cross over. But in other cases, they may need our assistance. A spirit chooses to stay in our physical realm for many reasons—passing suddenly, being taken before their time, having unfinished business, and even being emotional can play a role. All of these things can keep the spirit bound to Earth. You can help their soul transition into the light and continue their journey.

There are three basic steps to helping a spirit cross over. You must be aware that a lost soul can be dangerous, though. The longer a spirit stays trapped in one area, the angrier the spirit can become. Over time, an angry soul can become powerful and harmful to humans, but only in rare cases.

Step number one: you have to set boundaries. Reach out to a loved one who has passed to act as an angel or spirit guide—a person who you trusted from a previous life, perhaps a grandparent, parent, or sibling. It should be someone who offers good vibrational light, your protective energy. This should keep you safe from angry spirits or dark entities.

Wow, so I can help Jimmy and hopefully Annabelle. My grandmother passed away a few years ago—maybe I can summon her as my protecting angel. My mind raced with possibilities.

Step two: it's essential always to remember that the person you are speaking to was a real person once—ghosts have feelings, too. A spirit can be scared. You may think they are haunting you, but in reality, they are petrified of crossing over. You have to be the voice of reason and help them understand this is the best for all parties involved. Spirits don't understand time—they may not realize it's been a hundred years or longer since they have passed. You have *to help them understand what year it is, which may help push them to the other side. Two last things: don't forget to introduce yourself and reassure them it is safe to cross over; nothing terrible will happen to them when they do.*

*Step three: call upon their loved ones already on the other side—this is usually comforting, and the spirits will make the transition easier. You may not always see or hear the others you have summoned, but don't be discouraged! Pay attention to anything you notice as you offer support. You may feel in your heart that they are with you. If you require extra support, call on the Archangel Azrael, whose name means "Whom God helps." He's known as the angel who assists those who are dying and/or dead. Azrael can provide comfort to the dying and help lost souls cross over to the other side. His energy is empowering, but you may not know he is in your presence. You may notice a pale twinkling yellow light, letting you know his healing is at work.*

*Most importantly, don't forget to thank all the spirits who came to assist you. We don't want to upset the spirit world; you only want to help someone who needs your help.*

I was at a loss for words. I guess there is more to this spirit world stuff than I thought. It was getting late, and I knew Mother would check on me shortly. I sprang to my feet and dashed downstairs to get my teeth brushed. I learned this evening that I would need help from Donald Thornhill's deceased relatives. But I didn't know any of them or even who they were. Maybe Annabelle could help with that? Or I could find the answers in *The Thornhills of Pennsylvania* book that I still had to read. I guess reading that will have to wait until tomorrow. I rinsed my mouth and spat in the sink. I poked my head around the corner and wished my mom and dad a good night. They barely acknowledged me, being too engrossed in watching television.

I slowly made my way up the stairs, and the minute my head hit the pillow, I was out like a light.

Saturday morning came quickly. I had told Tom I would come to the store today around ten. I dashed downstairs for a quick bowl of Quisp. Those crunchy little spaceships tasted tremendous, and I polished off the cereal in record time. Quickly, I tossed my spoon and bowl into the sink, put the milk away, brushed my teeth, and strode back to my bedroom. I grabbed *The Thornhills of Pennsylvania* off my nightstand and started reading. The first few chapters were a little boring, so I tried to read the book in my best English accent to spice it up a bit. The book was about a wealthy family from Dartford, a suburb of London, England. The Thornhills came to America to expand their weapons business but found no war then, so they started a tool company named Sharp Edge Tools instead.

I noticed the family names and jotted them down—Rebecca, Donald's mother, and Richard, his father. He also had two brothers, one named Robert, and the other, Richard the second, named after his father. The boys were young when they moved to the United States. The family lived in upstate New York and had built a successful tool business. Donald grew up and went to New York State College and graduated with a degree in business. He worked with his father and brothers and learned the ins and outs of the tool business.

I skipped to the next chapter, which held nothing important, so I leafed through until I found what I was craving.

*Several years later, Donald was traveling through the hills of Pennsylvania when he spotted a beautiful area and a creek with crystal-clear water. The land was perfect, with plenty of woods and a small river to float the logs to his soon-to-be factory. With his father's and brothers' backing, they soon broke ground and built the factory and a few surrounding homes.*

*People came from all over to work at his factory, and the town grew. The small village was nestled in the mountains about a mile downstream from the factory. Because the mill was located in the hollows, they called the town Mill Hall. Everything was going according to plan. Then one day, while having lunch at the local diner, Donald met a young waitress named Annabelle, and she won his heart. But there was one problem—she was only sixteen, though Donald didn't seem to care. After all, he built the area and felt they owed him. Mill Hall might never have existed if it wasn't for the Thornhill family. It took him a few years, but with his persistence, he made Annabelle his wife.*

*Annabelle's family owed the bank a large sum of money, and Robert Thornhill paid off their debt as a gift for his younger brother's new in-laws. But it was not Annabelle's wish. It was an arranged marriage, and she was forced to marry Donald. Annabelle would be her husband's downfall, as Donald had a jealous side. He wondered if she truly loved him or if her heart belonged to another.*

*The marriage didn't last but a few years. One night, Donald came home to find another man in his house. He recognized the man as one of his employees from the factory. How could Annabelle? In a moment of rage, Donald struck him down. Then, he carried the man's body to the woods, where he would hide the evidence. When he returned home, he found his wife's lifeless body suspended from the ceiling—she had taken her own life. After several moments of grief, he did the only respectful thing he could think of—he carried her to the woods and buried her. That is the only logical explanation because their bodies were never found. Then he returned home and took his own life, leaving behind his only daughter, who was three at the time, and an illegitimate son he had with a woman named Samantha Smithers.*

*What?* I couldn't believe my eyes. Had I read that correctly? I looked again. I was stunned to learn Donald had a son, and his last name was Smithers.

# ELEVEN

I was in disbelief. Donald Thornhill had a son, and his last name was Smithers. Could Old Man Smithers be a relative? Did Tom know this? And if he did, why on earth hadn't he shared that with me? I thought our friendship was closer than that. I couldn't wait to call the group and tell them what I had learned—the excitement was killing me. But first, I needed to go to the store and talk to Tom.

I interrupted Mom while she was folding the laundry and told her that I was going to work and that I would see her later that afternoon. I raced upstairs, snatched my jacket, and returned to grab my bike. My mind was spinning. *How come no one ever talked about Thornhill's son?* I peddled faster as I descended the path to take a shortcut through the woods. I raced up a few small hills and back down again, then I popped a wheelie as I crested the top of an enormous mound. I increased my speed as I went down the other side and then banked a sharp left as I went into the turn at the bottom. I felt alive. My mind flashed. *If Old Man Smithers is a grandson or great-grandson of Donald*

*Thornhill, then he could be the missing piece of the puzzle we need to solve this riddle.*

I peddled faster, skirting the banks of the creek. Steam rising off the surface told me the air was colder than the water. I banked to the right as the path wound away from the stream. *I couldn't believe Tom had kept a secret from me after what I had shared with him last summer—opening the puzzle box and solving the riddle inside to find the cave, then introducing him to Annabelle, Jacob, and Jimmy. I would be upset if Tom knew that Smithers is a descendant of Thornhill. Why would he not tell me? Why was this eating me up inside?* I grew angrier the more I thought about this and peddled faster, which increased my speed. My mind raced with anger. I cleared the top of the next hill by a foot as my wheels soared through the air. The bike came down hard, and I slammed on my brakes in an attempt to stop, and that's when I noticed a tree down across the path. It was too late; I was coming in hot when I skidded into the trunk of the tree and rocketed over the top of the handlebars.

My head spun as I tried to place my hands before me to brace for impact. The cold, wet dirt and grass were all I remember as my body slammed to the ground, knocking the wind out of me. I must have blacked out for a few minutes, though I wasn't sure exactly how long I was out. My right wrist ached when I came to. I gingerly moved my hand up and down—that was a good sign; I didn't think it was broken. I felt a sharp pain in my left knee and above my eye. I rolled over and looked at my clothes. I had torn a hole in another pair of jeans. I knew right away that Mother was going to be upset. I felt a little jittery as I tried to stand. I glanced to the left, then to the right. An eerie feeling came over me as I looked around. I felt a set of eyes watching me.

"Is anyone there?" I yelled. Turning an ear to the forest, I listened intently. I hollered a little louder with no response.

Frustrated, I struggled to my feet and brushed myself off. I knew I'd be fine. I just needed a minute to gather my wits. I wiped my forehead and noticed a spot of blood on my sleeve. I was sure this would hurt more tomorrow than it did right now. I climbed back over the log and quickly looked at my bike—the front tire was flat, and the rim was bent. I guess I'd be pushing the bike the rest of the way. My head snapped to the left when I heard a grunt in the woods and the cracking of branches underfoot—something or someone was approaching. "Is anyone there?" I yelled louder. Only silence. It must be an animal, and I hoped it was not a large one, like a bear. I had already had one run-in with a bear in my life, and I didn't want another.

Another crack of a branch and a rustle of leaves sent fear through my body. I stood helpless against whatever was about to appear from the underbrush. I spun around and looked up at the trees. I didn't notice or hear any crows. That was a good sign, I guess. I forced my attention back to the mountain laurel that covered the ground and toward the small pine trees with much anticipation. A small branch gradually pushed forward. I gazed intently, my heart pounding out of my chest. Any moment now. Slowly, the branch moved forward, revealing a baby groundhog rooting around the underbrush for nuts or fallen berries. He appeared occupied with finding food and never glanced at me.

I rocked back on my heels, quite relieved to see the small rodent. Smiling, I picked up my bike and lifted it over the log, then climbed over myself. I limped toward the store, a little sore, but I would be alright—I was more worried about my bicycle than myself. After all, that was the only transportation I had.

The walk took forever, but finally, I pulled up alongside the road not far from the store. I could see it from where I stood. I wasn't sure how to approach Tom about what I had learned in the book. Straightforward was what my father always told us. "If you have something to ask, then say it," he always told Buck and me. That would probably be my best strategy. I just had to wait for the right moment.

I pushed my bike to the front of the store. Tom was standing near the window and spotted me. At first, he waved, but then his face went long. Scrambling, he threw the door open. "Johnny, are you alright?"

"Yeah, I'm fine; I had a little mishap on the way here," I mumbled, trying to downplay the accident.

"Come over here; let's take a look at you," he said. He placed a hand on my forehead and pushed my hair back to get a better look. He tilted my head from side to side, then glanced at my hands and wrist, turning each over a time or two. His eyes moved down to my knees, and he frowned. "I see you tore another pair of jeans."

"I know. My mom's going to kill me," I blurted out.

Tom smiled and pulled a handkerchief from his pocket to dab the blood from my face. "I think you're going to be just fine." He smiled. "Now, let's take a look at your bike." He pulled the bike into the garage bay, and I followed. "I think I can straighten the rim out enough for you to be able to ride. I'm sure I have some twenty-inch tubes that will fit inside your tire." He worked quickly, pulling the tire off and bending the rim with a bit of heat from his torch. In no time at all, the rim was straightened, and the tire and tube were installed. I could tell Tom had plenty of experience fixing bikes.

I thanked him and asked how much I owed him. Raising a hand, he told me to hush. Then he asked the right question, and I knew now was the right time to pounce. "How's school going this year?" Tom asked.

"It's going great. I love math and science, but I've been fascinated with local history."

"Hmm," he said while adding air to the tire. I watched as he installed the tire to the forks on the front of my bike. Tom placed a nut to secure the tire and rim to the spokes. With one last twist of the wrench, he gave the wheel a light spin. I noticed a slight wobble, but it was almost as good as new.

"I've been reading this book, *The Thornhills of Pennsylvania*, for class. It's a great story with lots of interesting facts."

Tom paused and looked at me, almost like he wanted to say something, but he didn't.

"I'm reading it for a class project. I have to write an essay for history. You know how that is?" Tom nodded, so I continued, "I found something interesting while reading. Did you know Donald Thornhill had a son?" Tom shot me a sidelong stare. He knew where I was going with this, but he said nothing. "Yeah, the book said he had a son named Bobby Smithers."

Tom stopped moving for a second. He started to open his mouth, then shut it. He turned the bike back over and pushed it toward me. "I think your bike's gonna be fine, but I would get a new rim soon," he suggested. "If you'd like, I can order one from the cycle shop."

I smiled. "That would be great, but I don't have any cash with me today unless you can deduct it from my pay?" I gave him a long face.

He smiled. "Sure, that won't be a problem." He thought he was out of the woods by changing subjects, but I had other plans.

"So, about the book I'm reading… Is Bobby Smithers related to Old Man Smithers?"

Tom frowned and let out a gasp of air. He paused, finally confirming what I was thinking. "Yes, Old Man Smithers' first name is Bobby—Bobby the third, to be exact."

I cracked a smile, a small victory for me. But now what? I knew the truth, but how did all this fit together? I needed to know all the facts. The bell rang as someone pulled their car up to the gas pumps. "Excuse me," Tom said as he approached the front door.

I watched as Tom pumped the gas, wondering what my next move would be. And my heart dropped when I realized that I didn't have one. None of this proved anything. I could only think of one question to ask. Tom finished cleaning the windshield, and I watched as the car pulled away. The bells above the door rang when Tom returned.

"We have a lot of work to get done. Can you start by sweeping the shop and taking out the trash?" Tom asked.

"Sure." I paused. "But can I ask you another question?" I didn't wait for Tom to answer. "Did you tell Old Man Smithers that we found a body in the cave?" I watched as Tom fidgeted around.

The air oozed out of Tom's lungs as my question left him speechless. Then the words I had longed to hear came out of his mouth. "Yes, I told Bob Smithers about the body in the cave. I explained everything—from the puzzle box to the body, even all three of our ghost friends." He paused. "I guess now there are only two." He frowned. "I'm sorry. I never meant to hurt anyone, especially Jimmy."

I felt a little joy knowing I was right, and I smiled. We discussed everything a little more and reviewed the details and what we had to do to fix everything. It wasn't long before Tom mentioned that we needed to get the store cleaned along with the shop. "Say no more." I moved away and grabbed the broom. I started to sweep the shop. Once I finished that task, I gathered the trash and boxes. My mind flashed back to our conversation. I fretted over telling the group because I knew Buck, Parker, and, most likely, Lexi would be upset that I talked to Tom before them.

A lot of things went through my mind on my way home. I felt thankful to have Tom in my life—he did a great job fixing the rim. The ride was pretty smooth, and I barely noticed the wobble. The other thing that stood out the most was how cold the temperature was getting. Winter was just around the corner, and if we didn't do something soon, we would have to wait until spring to help Jimmy.

# TWELVE

School and work kept me pretty busy, and winter was fast approaching. I briefly spoke with Buck about what Tom and I had discussed in the store. He said he mentioned it to Parker and Lexi, and everyone agreed that this would have to wait until spring. I guess no one was brave enough to go on an adventure in the middle of hunting season. The last thing we wanted was for someone to mistake us for a deer and take a shot while we were walking around the woods.

I reached out to Jimmy to no avail. I didn't understand why he wouldn't respond. The days and weeks passed, and still no answer. December arrived, and so did the snow. Before I realized it, the school was out for our annual holiday break. We had a pretty good snowstorm that dropped five or six inches on Christmas Eve. I always loved having snow for Christmas.

Buck, Parker, Lexi, Sara, and I were sitting in our family living room in front of the Christmas tree—a tradition we had started a few years before. Mother brought out some of her homemade hot cocoa, which tasted delicious.

"Thanks, Mrs. Malone," Lexi and Sara said in unison, and they both giggled. The summer dance events were behind us, and I was grateful for that. The minute Mother ducked out of the room, the lights flickered and became brighter on the tree. One by one, we stopped talking and turned our attention to it, sitting silent and wide-eyed. I think Lexi was the first to notice.

Sara scooted back a little and pulled in closer to me. I smiled. I was beginning to like it when she was close to me. The tree grew brighter, then faded, and then, out of nowhere, Jimmy's face appeared in the middle of the branches. The sizeable floating head slowly moved out of the tree and into the room. His face was huge, the size of a refrigerator. We all breathed a sigh of relief. He smiled and changed back to his complete figure. That was the first time I realized we were all aging, and Jimmy still had the same young look. It was hard to think that he had been gone for well over a year.

"Merry Christmas, Jimmy." I smiled.

He smiled back. "Merry Christmas to you all."

"How did you do that?" Buck asked.

"Do what?"

"Make your head so big."

"Oh, that… I've learned a couple of new tricks in the past few months. Annabelle has taught me a lot about being a ghost. She's been accommodating," he said, giving us a childish grin.

My curiosity was piqued. "What else can you do?"

He evaporated right in front of us. "Wait… Where'd he go?" Parker gasped.

"I'm right here," Jimmy whispered in Parker's ear, appearing directly behind him.

"That's pretty cool," Lexi said.

He disappeared again. We looked from right to left, and he was nowhere in the room. "Did he leave?" Sara asked.

A squeak resonated from under the tree. A white rat about the size of a small dog skidded out. The girls both jumped back and let out high-pitched screams. The sound was enough to terrify me.

"It's just me," the rat whispered.

"Is everything alright in there?" Father bellowed from the other room.

"We're fine, just horsing around," Buck hollered back.

Things quieted, and Jimmy transformed into a boy right before our eyes. "Sorry about that. I got caught up in the moment. It's not like I can walk around and do that to people all day. I mean, I could, but that would be downright cruel." He smirked.

Our heads nodded in agreement.

"So, what brings you here today?" I asked.

"I miss hanging out with you guys. It gets lonely… Most of the time, I watch from a distance. I don't know if I should show myself or not, and when I do, it drains me. I feel weak and need to rest. I sit and watch as time goes by while my spirit recharges."

I felt sorry for Jimmy. There was no other way to feel. "Is that why you don't always come when I call you?"

"Not exactly. I mean, I want to show myself and come and talk, but I can't. Take today, for example. I'll spend time with you guys, and then I'll need a few moments to recharge. But in reality, three or four human days will pass. The longer I stay visible, the longer it takes to recover. But that's my curse to bear."

"Wow, none of us knew that," I said as I looked around the room at the others, who confirmed my thoughts. "Does this apply to all ghosts?" I had to know. I was hatching a plan.

"It sure does, but the longer you've been a ghost, the more powerful you become. Take Annabelle, for instance; she can be visible for hours, unlike me, where I can show myself for only twenty or thirty minutes. And she recharges faster than I can, but I'm getting better at it."

"Does it suck your power when you're not visible? What happens when you only move an object? How does that affect you?"

"I feel my strength fade, but not as bad as when I show myself. That's the biggest drain on my soul." He smiled, and we watched him fade away.

One of the ornaments on the right side of the tree began to swing back and forth.

"Cool, neat trick." I smiled, totally jealous. "Okay, we'll ask you questions. If it's yes, move an ornament on the right; if no, move one on the left."

He moved the Christmas ball on the right side of the tree.

"Oh, do you ever go to the girls' locker room to watch them get undressed or check them out in the showers?" Parker grinned.

"Billy Parker," Lexi hissed, slapping Parker on the side of his head.

"Ouch," he screamed back. One of the ornaments on the left side started to swing.

Sara glared at her older brother with much disappointment until he finally apologized.

"Can we get on with this?" Lexi asked.

"Yes, let's move on." Buck frowned at Parker and sucker punched him in the arm—to impress Lexi, I'm sure. Out of the corner of my eye, I noticed Buck wink.

"Do you follow us around?" I asked, and the ornament on the right side started to swing.

"Did you come here to ask us for help?" Again, one of the ornaments on the right began to swing.

I looked directly at the tree as if I was looking into Jimmy's eyes. "I've finished reading the books about how to cross a spirit over. I think I know how we can do this. Would you like us to help you cross over?"

The seconds ticked by, and none of the ornaments moved. "Jimmy? Are you still here?" I noticed the ball on the right move a little.

"Do you want us to help you cross over to the other side?"

I watched and waited with great anticipation. Finally, after ten or fifteen seconds, one of the balls on the right side of the tree swung back and forth. I smiled. Deep inside, I knew it was the right thing to do. Jimmy reappeared. "When do you plan to do this?"

That was the tricky question. "Save your strength and disappear. Let me work out some details, and I'll let you know. I'm pretty sure it will be spring or early summer before we can act on our plan."

Jimmy nodded and gave us a quick smile. "What do you need from me?"

Lexi, Sara, Parker, and Buck faced me. They knew what I was about to ask. "I-I need," I sputtered. "I need … to know where your body's located." I grimaced as the words rolled off my tongue.

"I have one favor to ask of you. I want Annabelle to cross over, and that nasty old man of hers needs to go too.

I don't care if they go up or down; I want them removed from this Earth. If you can help me, I'll show you where my body is located." Jimmy frowned. We looked at each other for a few seconds before he vanished again.

We each asked a few more questions after that. However, none of the ornaments on the right or left moved. I couldn't help but wonder if he was upset because we had to wait until spring or if maybe he was tired and needed to rest.

I wasn't sure how we would send Annabelle or Donald Thornhill to the other side, but I was going to try for Jimmy's sake.

I didn't see or hear from Jimmy during the rest of the Christmas break. I spent my spare time re-reading the books, again and again, each time making notes. I wanted to make sure I had my facts straight.

Outside, the wind howled, and the rain continued to pelt down on the house. My mind flashed to Sara. I picked up my phone, and still no text, which was unlike her. Frustrated, I sent her a text.

[Johnny: Are you okay?]

Storms like this can create long nights at the hospital. She loved what she did, and I guess that's what gave me comfort. I was worried but couldn't let the boys see that on my face; I smiled.

"Dad, Earth to Dad… Hello, are you here?" Zack asked.

"Sorry, I was thinking about your mother. I'm allowed to do that, right?" Both boys nodded with approval.

"So, were you able to cross Jimmy over?" Daniel asked.

"I think you are jumping ahead a bit, right?"

They nodded again. I looked at our candles and told each of the boys to grab another candle from the box before I continued my story. As much as I enjoyed telling the boys my life story, I hoped the power would soon return.

After lighting new candles, we were ready for me to finish my story.

# THIRTEEN

That was one of the roughest winters I can remember. Snowstorm after snowstorm, they came quickly and often. Once April arrived and spring was just around the corner, it gave us all something to look forward to.

Buck and I waited for Scooter and Todd. We planned to meet Parker at his house since he lived a minute from the ax factory dam. There was a knock at the door, and Buck answered while I helped Mother clean the breakfast dishes. When I turned around, I saw Todd standing before me, wearing a new fishing vest. I remember he didn't own any fishing or camping equipment when he first moved here from the big city, but now he asks for those items for birthdays and holidays.

I dried the last dish, placed it in the cabinet, and kissed Mother on the cheek. I blasted upstairs to grab my jacket, then dashed to the basement where Buck and Todd studied our fishing gear. A knock pounded on the door. Scooter must have seen the basement light on and decided to go around to the back instead.

Buck opened the door, and I was right. Scooter beamed, holding his new tackle box and a shiny new rod and reel. "Wow, nice gear," I said, sounding a little jealous. He was an only child, and his parents spoiled him. Sometimes I wished I was an only child, but I couldn't imagine life without my brother.

"Dad bought me this for Christmas. I can't wait to use it," he said, sporting a mile-long grin. Then Scooter handed Todd his old fishing pole, and his smile grew wider. "It's all yours. I think you'll like it."

"I-I'm not sure what to say." A happy tear formed in Todd's eye. "Thank you."

"It's cool, dude." Scooter smiled, slapping Todd on the shoulder, and turned to the door. We grabbed our gear, and we trekked to Parker's house. Buck and Todd walked ahead, with Scooter and me bringing up the rear. There was nothing better than the opening day of fishing season. I couldn't wait to cast my line in the water. My mind wandered back to that summer two years ago when Jimmy was with us. It seemed odd that he wasn't tagging along. I hoped he would make an appearance today.

Scooter and I had recently turned fifteen. I was glad he was finally out of that clumsy, awkward stage he went through as a kid. He even walked with more confidence. We walked up the stairs and across the wooden porch. The door opened before we had a chance to knock. Parker was ready to go and closed the door behind him. We crossed the road and walked down the embankment toward the dam. The air was cool, and a layer of fog hung over the water, hindering our visibility. There was an eerie feeling about this place in the morning. The water roared over the broken section of the dam. I didn't want to walk in that direction — we lost

Jimmy there. I wasn't sure any of us had been to that side of the dam since that terrible day.

Parker turned right, steering us toward the dirt path that skirted Big Fishing Creek. The grass and weeds were brown and brittle underfoot. The ground was no longer frozen, and the recent snow had melted. Some areas were still mushy and our shoes sank into the mud. We walked for five or ten minutes until we cleared the bend in the creek. I flashed back to when three deer jumped across our path and Jimmy and Parker arguing that day. A smile crossed my face. Those were great times. Many times, we spotted muskrats, beavers, or porcupines. I remembered a time when we found a copperhead snake. The snake was still too cold to move, so we jabbed him with sticks.

A shadow raced across the path. My head popped up to attention. *I need to stay on my toes.* That was odd. The sun hadn't cleared the top of the mountain yet, so how could I see a shadow? My mind must have been playing tricks on me. I called out to Jimmy in case he was with us, but he never answered.

"Dude, let's not talk about him, okay?" Scooter whispered to me.

"Sorry," I replied. Scooter was right—my mind was obsessed with Jimmy. Was I wrong about that? Maybe I was ridiculous to think we could help him. After all, I was still a kid.

Scooter and I heard some quiet talking as we made our way past the older boys, who had stopped. I noticed Parker, Todd, and Buck edge their way down over the bank and pull up close to the water.

"We're going above the rapids," I said to Buck.

"Chase them this way." He chuckled, and we walked farther upstream.

A light breeze rolled off the water. We stopped above the rapids, where the water flowed steadily yet remained relatively calm. Scooter went another twenty feet above me. This looked like the perfect spot to fish. I set my gear down and pulled open my container of worms, grateful that Buck and I had gathered them earlier in the week. Pulling a giant fat worm out, I inched him onto my hook. Scooter was using the shiny new lure his dad had bought him, but I preferred natural bait over the artificial kind—I was a little old-fashioned that way. I pulled the rod back over my head and snapped it forward as I released the reel—my line stretched out over the creek before plopping into the water.

I sat down on an old stump, which happened to be conveniently sitting next to the water. I watched my line slowly drift downstream and began to reel it in at a slow, steady pace. I repeated this process over and over that morning. A commotion broke out downstream. I heard a bunch of hooting and hollering. The fish weren't biting, at least not for me. I guess the others were having better luck catching them. Scooter seemed to be having a better day than me, too. Maybe it was his shiny new lure.

The sun cleared the top of the mountain as I continued to cast my line out; I was just relaxing and enjoying the morning. I carefully listened as the woods came to life— bees buzzing in the nearby bushes, birds chirping in the distance. *What a glorious morning this was turning out to be!*

Suddenly my line jerked, and my attention now focused on the water. My line jumped again, only this time, it was a quick tug. I pulled back to set the hook in the fish's mouth, and the fight was on. The fish dipped to the right and then took a hard left. I kept the line tight and worked the reel as I brought it closer to shore. I caught sight of the fish, and something seemed a little odd. It looked long and thin, almost like a snake. I was petrified. "Scooter," I hollered, "bring the net, quick!" I kept the line tight and reeled slower, giving Scooter time to reel his line to shore, grab the net, and bring it to me. Footsteps quickly approached, and in a flash, Scooter stood by my side. He balanced beside me and stretched the six-foot pole and net out over the water. I could see the excitement written all over his face about what I might pull out of the water.

We stared at the water following the fight as my line moved around—whatever I hooked seemed to be tiring. I pulled my rod back and reeled in harder. I squinted to see if I could get a better look. Crap, it was an eel—just my luck. My day went from bad to worse in seconds. Eels were not loveable creatures. They could get large, almost the size of an adult's arm. If you pulled an eel from the water, it'd wrap around the rod and ruin your line; sometimes, it even broke the rod. Worse, they would bite when you tried to remove the hook. They had large razor-sharp teeth. Needless to say, I didn't want to make a trip to the hospital.

"Cut the line! Cut the line!" I chanted.

Scooter froze. His arm stretched out, still holding the net.

"Cut the line!" I screamed, and the seconds passed. I stopped reeling and watched it thrash around in the water.

The rustling of footsteps rapidly approached from behind, and in a flash, Buck was standing next to me. He reached down, unfastened his knife from his holster, pulled it out, and waved the blade in front of me in one swift motion. He sliced the line and set the eel free to enjoy the worm it wanted for breakfast. My rod sprang up, and I jerked backward, almost tripping. Somehow, I managed to stay on my feet.

It was instant gratification for Buck. I could see his mile-wide smile. My brother had come to my rescue. Something was wrong. The eel didn't swim away; it was coming closer to the shore. If my eyes were not deceiving me, the eel was growing. The enjoyment of setting it free had vanished. I stepped back, tripping over the log and landing on my butt.

"Parker!" Buck shouted.

As the words left his mouth, Parker and Todd appeared out of nowhere. The eel continued to grow, pulling itself onto the shore. Todd grabbed a long, thin stick that was lying on the riverbank. He thrust it forward at the serpent's head. The eel had grown four or five times its normal size and was starting to stand when the head changed into human form—Donald Thornhill!

I flashed back to Christmas Eve when Jimmy turned himself into a rat. The old man had done the same. He towered before us, face to face, peering down as we looked on. My head spun; I felt dizzy and afraid. I froze. There was no place to hide from this ghost.

"Boys, boys, boys," he hissed and shook his head. Scooter moved away from the shore but still held the net before him. Only this time, he pointed the fishing net directly at the large ghost head attached to an eel's body.

"You're no match for me, boys," he snarled.

"Back up," Parker said as he pulled the knife from its sleeve. He waved it before him, and Buck moved to his side and did the same. Todd joined, holding the large stick. I got to my feet and grabbed the closest thing I could find—a large rock.

Donald Thornhill smiled. "I'm a ghost… You can't cut or stick me; the rock will pass through me." He turned to Scooter. "And you can't put a net over me," he said and laughed.

"Leave us alone," Parker yelled.

"I will," he sighed, "if you leave me and my family alone." His voice grew louder. "Stop plotting and planning, and no more séances. Do you understand?" he warned.

"You don't own them—"

"Silence," he yelled. "Listen, boys. Heed my warning— leave us alone, or you will all pay the price." Then, he vanished.

"Did that just happen?" Todd asked.

"I think so," Buck and Parker replied simultaneously.

None of us wanted to call it quits for the day, but we did anyway. We packed up and hiked back to Parker's house. I hoped the girls would be home. We needed to talk and see if there was a way to reach Jimmy without the old man knowing.

# FOURTEEN

We arrived at Parker's house shortly after the incident at the creek. We were in luck. Sara and Lexi were home, and their parents had gone to town but would return at any time. We explained to the girls what had happened while we were fishing. Lexi suggested we go upstairs so we could have some privacy. We filed in line and made our way up the creaky stairs and into the attic.

"I've been doing a little research about evil spirits," Lexi said.

"You can read?" Buck snickered.

"Yes, I can read." She smiled back while slapping him on the arm.

"Ouch, you don't have to hit so hard," he replied.

"Don't be a baby," Parker snorted, high-fiving his sister.

"Can we get down to business? I'm tired of this ghost haunting us. The question is, how do we get rid of him?" I pleaded.

The temperature plummeted, and I could see my breath in the air. We nervously looked around the room—we knew what would happen. We didn't know who was going to show up. A bright light streamed out from the old chair in the corner of the room. My gaze fixed on it as the light grew in brightness and size. I wasn't sure what to think, what to believe, or how scared I should be. I glanced at Sara when she grabbed my hand. I smiled and tried to reassure her that everything would be alright.

The light burst from the chair and quickly flew across the room in a whirl. "Hi, guys," Jimmy yelled as he spun to face us.

A sigh of relief rushed over us. "Don't do that," I whispered, trying to find my voice.

"Something I've been practicing," he said proudly.

"I didn't know you could make the temperature drop." Parker marveled.

Jimmy smiled. "You liked that, did ya? Annabelle taught me."

"We're losing focus," Lexi said as she lit several incense sticks before her. "I've been reading about warding off evil spirits. They say if you light incense, it will help ward off the negativity." She smiled.

"You're right; I don't like the smell, but I'm not evil," Jimmy reminded us. "There is one thing you could use, and that's amethyst crystals. I heard they have healing and cleansing powers, not to mention their protective powers will keep anything negative from coming near. It's called the stone of the spirit." Jimmy looked proud of himself. "Oh, there are a few other stones, like rose quartz or black tourmaline."

"What kind of rocks are they?" I asked.

"I'm not sure, but Annabelle told me to avoid them. I don't think I'm supposed to tell you that."

"Well, that was not very helpful," Parker mumbled.

"Wait a minute… I think this could be helpful. What if we went to the cave and Jimmy met us there? Then he could show us how he felt around certain rocks. We could gather the stones and keep them in our pockets. It could ward off the evil spirits, like the old man," I suggested.

"It sounds like a stupid idea." Buck grunted.

"I agree," Parker said. That, along with Lexi's wry grin and nod, told me this might not be a good plan.

"Just a thought," I said, dismissing the idea for now. I brought Jimmy up to speed. He had no clue about the ordeal we had encountered along the creek.

"Here's what you need to do," Jimmy explained, and we listened intently. "First, we need to find Annabelle's remains, dig them up, and return them to the cemetery. Then we need to do the same with Donald's remains."

"How do we do that? Not to mention that we don't even know where the bodies are located," Parker snarled at Jimmy.

"Easy, I think I have a good idea where Annabelle's remains might be. She favors this one spot—I think she's guarding something. I also might know where the old man's buried, but I think he's waiting for someone to join him before he goes."

"So, are you saying that if we take Annabelle's body and put it with Donald's, he will leave? Or will they both leave?" a meek voice asked.

I forgot Scooter was sitting on the opposite side of me. He was always shy and awkward in these types of situations. I couldn't help the smile that grew on my face.

"I think so," Jimmy said with a hint of doubt in his voice.

"What if it doesn't work?" Todd asked.

Jimmy shrugged his shoulders. "It should, but maybe you can confirm that in a book or something."

"I did read something about that in the book Johnny gave me," Sara hinted.

"I remember that. If we bury her remains properly next to him, that fulfills his heart's desire, and Donald should cross over. And laying her body to rest should also send her to the other side. I don't care where they go as long as they're gone," I said.

"Do you mean Heaven or Hell?" Todd asked.

"What does it matter?" I asked.

"I guess it doesn't, but it might to our ghosts."

"I agree, but I can't worry about that. We need to get Annabelle and Donald out of here," I said.

"I agree, and if it works, then we should try it," Lexi said.

Buck nodded, and Parker did the same. Todd, Sara, and I all turned toward Scooter, who, after a long pause, finally gave the nod.

"So, what's next?" I looked at the blank faces in the room. "Where do we find the bodies?" Still no response. "And when we locate them, how do we move them?"

"Tom will help," Jimmy said. "Listen, let me find out where she's buried, and I'll be in touch." We all watched and waved as he slowly faded away. The temperature warmed and quickly returned to normal.

"Time to eat," Parker announced.

I watched as the three older boys bounced to their feet and marched down the stairs to raid the kitchen. Lexi and Sara looked nervous when I heard Scooter say, "We need to do this."

"What about Jimmy?" Sara asked.

"Jimmy promised me, in so many words, that if we could get rid of the older ghosts, he would show me where his body's located. Then we could steer the authorities to the location. Once Jimmy is properly buried, he should cross over. At least, that's what he said." I frowned. The thought of Jimmy going away forever always saddened me, but I knew it was for the best. "I'll talk to Tom and see if he'll help…" I grimaced, knowing this was not going to be an easy conversation.

"Are we done?" Scooter asked.

"I think so," I replied.

Before the words flew out of my mouth, Scooter was already heading for the door. I bounced to my feet and waited on the girls as we strode toward the stairs, anxious to see what tomorrow would bring.

# FIFTEEN

I lunged out of bed the following morning, bolted downstairs, ate breakfast, dressed, and said my goodbyes. Then I slowly rode my bike to the general store to chat with Tom. I was not looking forward to having this conversation. I'm not sure why I was so nervous. Tom and I had been through a lot, but we were also friends. I knew I could talk to him about anything. I guess it was a nagging feeling that I was still a kid, and he was an adult, not to mention my boss.

I pulled in and parked my bike around the back. The store was busy. I guess my questions would have to wait. Tom was in and out of the store all morning, pumping gas and cleaning windshields. I grabbed my broom, started sweeping, and picked up any garbage I could see. He had a few boxes of new candy sitting behind the counter, so I pulled the plastic wrap off the boxes, priced each item, and placed them on the shelf. From time to time, the bells above the door would chime, followed by someone looking to buy a product from the store. I recognized some of the folks who entered. One was an elderly, gray-haired lady named

Mary Sampsell; I'd shoveled snow off her driveway a few times. Another was Mr. Milton, who ran the cycle shop up the road from our house.

I was glad Tom had taken the time to teach me how to use the cash register. It made me feel important because I knew he trusted me with the money. Also, I was able to offer more help on a morning like this.

I couldn't wait until I came of age and could learn how to drive. Tom had told me that when I started to drive, he would show me how to close the store and let me work alone in the evenings. I'm sure Tom could use the break. His life was the store, and he didn't seem to have much of anything else—I don't think he even had a girlfriend. I couldn't imagine how lonely he must have been.

The church crowd slowed shortly after lunch, and I knew if I was going to get my chance to talk to Tom, now seemed like the perfect opportunity. "Hey, Tom, can we talk for a minute?"

"Sure, but before I forget, thanks for your help this morning; you arrived in the nick of time. I needed your assistance today."

A sense of pride washed over me. "Thank you."

"I did a quick tally, and we might be able to close early today. I love spring; it gets folks out and about, which means more business for me." Tom smiled again. "Oh, you said you had something you wanted to talk about?"

"Yes, I do." My words came out shaky and nervous. My palms were sweaty.

"If we close early, I might have time to finish the book I'm reading," Tom said.

"Oh, what are you reading?" I had to ask because I loved a good story, and it would be rude not to ask.

"I'm reading *The Hobbit* by J. R. R. Tolkien. Fascinating story, with lots of strange creatures and a place called Middle-earth." He beamed.

"I thought you read that before."

"I have, but when you love a story as I do, you sometimes find yourself reading it repeatedly. Have you read any good books lately?"

"Yes." Now was my chance to get back on topic. "I finished two books recently, both by the same author, Gerald Dupickle. Have you heard of him?" Tom gave me a meaningful look and then shrugged his shoulders. I didn't expect him to know the author unless he happened to be researching ghosts. "One story was about a ghost and evil spirits, and the other was about how to cross them over."

Tom shot me a funny look. "Why are you reading that nonsense?" he snarled.

Ah, finally. "Well," I took a deep breath, "Jimmy needs our help. And I thought if I knew enough about how to cross him over, I could help him. He wants to move on; did you know that?" Tom stood there, his eyes wide and mouth open as he gazed at me. "Tom, did I say something wrong?"

"No, no, not at all." He wrinkled his nose a bit and had a puzzled look on his face. "Is this what you wanted to talk to me about?"

"Ah, yes…" I inhaled and then let out a deep breath. "I need your help, Tom."

"No, I'm done with all this ghost nonsense," he whispered as if we were standing in a large crowd, and he wanted no one else to hear.

"You and I know they're real," I countered. "I spoke with Jimmy; he needs our help, and so does Annabelle." I frowned. I knew this would get him. After all, Annabelle was his great-great-great-grandmother or something like that. I couldn't remember the exact number of *greats*.

Tom lowered himself down to the chair behind the counter. I pulled over a milkcrate and sat down in front of him. "Will you at least hear me out?"

Tom nodded; he knew it was futile to try to stop me. When I set my mind to something, I wouldn't let it go.

I explained what we needed to do and what the others and I had discussed in the attic. There was only one thing that we didn't know, and I was hoping Tom could help with that. We talked for a few minutes, and eventually, he seemed to be on board. I only had one last question, and this would be the toughest of all. "Tom, we don't know where Annabelle's buried, but I think there's someone who could help with that…" Tom looked baffled. "Old Man Smithers," I blurted out. "He's the key."

"What?"

"Yes, Old Man Smithers… The book indicates he's part of the Thornhill family. I'm sure he could ask Donald Thornhill where he buried the body—"

"Wow," he cut in. "This is preposterous. You expect me to run over to Bob's house and ask him to speak to a ghost? I can imagine it now. "Oh, hi, Bob. Can you ask Donald where he buried Annabelle's body?" he mocked me.

"No… I mean…" I was unsure for a moment and finally found the right words. "Yeah, I do. That sounds about right. But I'll be there to help."

"I didn't think you and Bob were friends. Wait, you're not!" he shouted. "How in the world am I going to get him to help us?"

"Tom," I retorted, "hear me out. Invite yourself over and bring me with you. I can have Jimmy show up, and we can explain everything."

Tom rubbed his head in frustration. "You're insane. This is a crazy idea."

"Is it?" I rebutted. "Please, Tom, please." I made the saddest face I knew how.

"Ah, for crying out loud." He stood up and walked around the desk and towered over me. With his hands on his hips, I heard the words I wanted to hear. "I can't believe I'm going to do this."

I had this rush of gratification wash over me. "Yes!" I jumped up, wrapped my arms around him, and hugged him. I surprised Tom with affection, and I think I surprised myself, too. "You won't regret this. We might be able to put an end to all these hauntings."

"When do you want to go to Bob's?"

I beamed. "Tonight."

"Let me see if he's busy this evening. We can close around five, grab a bite to eat, and go over to talk." He placed his hands on his hips and walked in a circle. "I promise you nothing more than that, Johnny."

"Deal." The bells rang at the gas pump, and Tom pushed the door open and went outside to help. He looked back once and slightly shook his head. I knew this was the last thing he wanted to do, but I was glad he would help. Now I needed Jimmy to help me. "Jimmy, can you hear me?" I looked around, and nothing happened. "Please, Jimmy, we need to talk. I need your help."

The minutes passed, and still no Jimmy. Then I heard Tom enter the store, and he was talking to someone—a voice I knew all too well. I grabbed the garbage can from behind the desk and opened the door. I didn't want Todd's mom to think I was hiding in the office. "Hi, Mrs. Hanson." She was a tall, middle-aged woman with some of the prettiest eyes I'd ever seen. No, I didn't have a crush on her; she just had pretty eyes.

She picked up a few groceries, and Tom rang up the purchase on the register. She smiled and waved as Tom carried the bags out to her car. I didn't say anything as she left the store. I only watched to make sure the coast was clear. I turned around and went back into the office. "Jimmy, are you here?" Still nothing. Dang it, this was frustrating. "Jimmy, if you can hear me, please show up at Old Man Smithers' house around five-thirty or six this evening."

# SIXTEEN

I fumbled around, trying to stay busy, and watched the clock. The ticking sound was nearly deafening to me and my jumbled nerves. I didn't think this day was ever going to end. Much to my surprise—after walking laps in and out of the aisles—five o'clock finally arrived. It was about five minutes until five when Tom told me to lock things up. That was music to my ears. I watched him pull two Pepsis from the cooler and motion toward the potato chip rack. Without hesitation, I wrapped my hand around the last bag of Middleswarth barbeque-flavored potato chips—a Pennsylvania favorite.

I pushed the door open, and Tom locked the door behind us. We walked to the side of the building where Tom kept his 1972 Chrysler. I opened the passenger door and got inside. I opened the chips and rammed my hand inside the bag. I couldn't wait for the barbeque flavor to hit my tongue.

Tom shot me a stern look. "You better not make a mess in my car, or you'll be cleaning it."

"I'll be careful, promise." I raised my hand to form a cross over my chest. It was hopeless because I knew immediately that I'd have to come by the store tomorrow and vacuum out the car. I slid a few more chips into my mouth and savored the flavor. My timing was perfect. I polished off the bag as Tom turned down the long gravel road that was the entrance to Bob Smithers' property. I started to fidget in my seat.

"Are you alright?"

"Yeah, sure. It's... he's a mean old man."

"You look a little green if you ask me." Tom smiled. "Everything's going to be fine. Bob's not as bad as you kids make him out to be."

"Well, the last time I saw him, he had a rifle in his hands and was firing buckshot in the air to scare me off."

He grinned. "Did it work?"

"Yeah, of course, it did."

"Well, I guess you shouldn't be snooping around his property, now, should you?"

"We weren't—" The car rolled to a stop a few yards from Bob Smithers' front porch, and the rest of my explanation died in my throat. Tom opened his door and started to walk. He turned and motioned for me, and I saw him mouth the words, "Are you coming?" I reached for the handle and pulled up, then pushed the door open. I had never been inside Bob's place. I wondered what I would see. I expected his house to be messy, with dead bodies stuffed in the closets.

I snapped back to reality when his dog started to bark. I scampered over to stand behind Tom—I didn't want Bob to see me when he looked out the window. The handle began to turn, and the door slowly opened.

"Hi, Tom, a pleasant surprise. Come on in." He stepped aside to allow Tom access to the doorway. Nervously, I placed one foot on the step and then the other. I didn't want to be too far behind Tom. I watched as Tom bent down to play with the dog. Bob Smithers shot me the evil eye and watched every step I took. The door slammed behind me. My heart was racing. I think I would rather face the ghost of Robert Thornhill than be inside Bob Smithers' home. My throat was dry. I swallowed hard. I wasn't sure I would be able to talk.

"Why'd you bring that bucket of nuts with you?" Bob chuckled as he looked at me.

"Well, we sort of need to talk to you about something," Tom explained.

"What's he done now? Stole something from me? Didja?" He glowered at me.

"No sir, we need your help," I whispered as I looked at the floor.

I watched as Bob tilted his head to the side, looking puzzled. I'm sure he was wondering what I was doing at his place. I glanced around the house, and much to my surprise, it was lovely—clean and cozy. I was impressed and didn't expect what I was seeing. I guess he cared about his place after all.

"Can I offer you something to drink?"

"Oh, you're asking me?" I was stunned. "I'm fine. I just finished my soda, but thank you, sir."

"Well, at least the boy has manners. I guess that's why you let him work in your store."

"He's very helpful and good with the customers," Tom replied.

"I'm happy for you, Tom. I know you didn't come over here to chit-chat. Anyway, let's cut to the chase, shall we? Come on, boy, spit it out. What do ya need from me, Johnny?"

I glanced at Old Man Smithers and cleared my throat. "Do you know anything about the cave at the top of the mountain, the one behind the Parkers' house?" I wasn't sure where that question came from; I guess it was still fresh on my mind. I wanted to know who removed Jacob's body. For a second, I thought he was going to go ballistic. He rolled his eyes and scrunched his face. Bob looked like someone who was about to explode.

He gave a quick grin, and his face slowly returned to normal. "I like that, a young man who isn't afraid to ask the tough questions. I'm impressed, Johnny." He nodded and gave me a deep, dark stare. "Yes, I know about the cave. Tom told me this cockamamie story about you boys finding a cave, a dead body, and ghosts." He chuckled. "So, I had to check it out for myself. And much to my surprise, it was all true, just as Tom had described it. I found the cavern on the left side of the tunnel, as Tom had mentioned. I spotted the loose dirt and knew this had to be the spot. I yanked a folding shovel from my pack and dug him up. First, I found the puzzle box—an awe-inspiring piece of woodwork, I might add. Next, I found the body. I wrapped him in a fresh blanket and stuffed it best I could into a large duffle bag. It was a good thing I had brought those things with me."

Our mouths were agape as Bob continued, "I was thrilled this was not one of Tom's fantasies. I had my doubts at first. Then I made my way back down the mountain, stuffed everything into my car's trunk, and went straight to the cemetery. I figured whoever this person was deserved a better place to rest than a dusty, old cave."

"It was Jacob," I chimed in.

"Who's Jacob?"

"According to the old legends, he's the factory worker who had an affair with Annabelle, Donald Thornhill's wife."

"No, it was just a body. It could have come from anywhere," Bob said.

"That's not true. Tom and I know those remains belong to Jacob," I said.

Bob scrunched up his face again. He looked annoyed about something. "Crap," he whispered to himself.

"What's wrong?" Tom asked.

Tom already knew what was eating Bob, and I did, too… if what I read in the book was correct about the Thornhill family.

"Nothing," he managed to say through gritted teeth. "Ah hell, I've heard the legends, and the last thing I wanted to do was help that poor sap."

"But you did, which was nice of you," I said. I heard Bob sigh. "I want you to know that Jacob crossed over, which greatly upset Annabelle. You should take some comfort in that."

"Stop it. I don't believe in ghosts," Bob barked.

"I'm telling the truth," I said, and Tom nodded in agreement.

"Well, if ghosts do exist, then prove it… make one appear right now. If you can't, it's time for you to go."

"It's not that easy, and I'm sure you know that." I was a bit frustrated. I was counting on Jimmy to make an appearance, but I never heard back from him, so I had doubts he would show. And if I couldn't get a ghost to appear, how would I get Bob to believe us? "Jimmy, can you hear me? Please, Jimmy, I need you to show yourself," I begged, hoping Jimmy would show. A few minutes passed, and Tom and Bob looked around the room. Nothing, no Jimmy, no ghost, no nothing. How disappointing. But it made sense—Jimmy and I had never been inside Bob Smithers' house. Maybe he couldn't come into the house.

"Listen, I'm sure you thought you saw something in the cave that day. I agree it's a spooky place, but whatever you think you saw was a reflection or something like that, not a ghost." Bob shrugged.

"I know what I saw. If you have the puzzle box, I'll show you what it showed us," I said in desperation.

"I didn't keep the box—I buried it with the body."

"Liar," a voice barked from the other side of the room. I watched Bob's dog cower and crawl behind the sofa to hide.

Bob spun around, but there was no one there. "Who's there?"

A ghostly white vapor began to appear. It was coalescing, slowly, into the form of a young man. Bob took a few steps back and stumbled, landing in the seated position on the couch. Tom quickly moved beside Bob and laid a hand on his shoulder for comfort. "It's alright, Bob; no one will hurt you; I promise."

"This can't be." He rubbed his eyes. "No way, you slipped something into my drink. You had to. This can't be happening. Ghosts don't exist." He trembled.

Jimmy floated toward us, then sent a chill across the room, dropping the temperature about ten degrees. I shivered at the sudden drop. Bob's eyes widened in disbelief. I think Jimmy was beginning to like some of the tricks he could perform.

"You have the puzzle box in your closet," Jimmy said.

"I don't! I swear," Bob pleaded.

"Don't lie to me!" Jimmy roared. "I know things, and I see things you can't imagine. Since I'm here, Johnny won't need the box to prove that ghosts exist, but don't deny that you have the puzzle box when I know you do."

I was impressed by Jimmy's actions and timing. He had waited for the right moment to make his appearance. He hovered over the couch; he was gazing at Bob and Tom. "I need to know where Annabelle's body's buried," Jimmy said matter-of-factly.

"How, ah… how would I know that?" Bob stuttered.

"You can ask Donald Thornhill."

"Donald, who?"

If a ghost could have a color other than white, Jimmy's face would have turned beet red. "I'm going to go berserk and hurt you if you lie to me again," he threatened.

"Jimmy, calm down," I said, motioning with my hands, but he ignored me.

"I'm sorry, I don't know any Donald Thornhill," Bob whimpered.

"Wasn't he your great-great-grandpa?"

"Ah," Bob hesitated, "I think so, but I never met him. He died a long time ago."

"Yes, he did. You can ask him where Annabelle's buried. If you call his name, he will answer. I'm sure he'll tell you."

"Why would he tell me anything? And why is this so important?"

"Tell him if we have her remains, we can help him and Annabelle reunite, just like he always dreamed," Jimmy smirked.

"I-I-I'm not sure what to say."

"Don't push your luck," Jimmy hissed. "I'm tired of the games. I'm tired of the way you treated me when I was alive. It's time to make up for all your mistakes and learn what I need to know before something bad happens to you or your little dog." Jimmy began to flicker out.

"Jimmy, no need for threats—" But he was gone before I finished. I guess he was frustrated with all the drama between Donald Thornhill and Annabelle. Part of me didn't blame him. I turned my attention back to the couch where Tom was trying to calm Bob down. I felt terrible for the old man—seeing a ghost for the first time was a lot to take in. I remembered how I felt that day in the cave.

"Bob," I said calmly, "you just saw a ghost. It wasn't a trick; it happened. Jimmy's right. We need your help, and only you can do this."

Bob sat up, his eyes glazed over. He glanced at me, then back to Tom. It was an awkward moment. I wanted to tell him *I told you so*, but I kept my mouth shut for once. He scrunched his nose a bit and cocked an eyebrow at me. Slowly, he turned and whispered something in Tom's ear.

"Johnny, would you mind waiting outside?" Tom asked.

For a moment, I thought he would say yes. Now, my hope relied on Tom convincing Bob to help us. Jimmy's threat was pretty straightforward: *help us or pay the consequences*. I didn't see where Bob had much of choice.

I pushed myself to my feet. "I'm sorry, Mr. Smithers; I didn't mean to frighten you." His head bobbed, so I took the nod to mean he was alright. I slid my jacket back over my arms and went to the door. I stopped for a second to look over my shoulder, then pushed the door open and plopped my butt down on the front porch steps.

# SEVENTEEN

I sat on the porch and stared at the sky. Clouds blocked most of the stars; only a sliver of the moon shone across the dark evening sky. *Now I know why Parker always gazes at the stars—they are beautiful. Is there life out there? If ghosts exist, then I guess the possibility of aliens could be genuine, too. What wonders await us?* My mind wandered, and then I heard murmurs from inside the house. I wondered why Bob didn't freak out and go nuts when Jimmy showed up. Bob's response appeared rehearsed, or was that just me being cynical? It was like he had seen a ghost before, but where? Had Annabelle tried to stop him from taking Jacob's remains? I guess I'll never know the answer to those questions. I felt Bob was hiding something.

I was curious about their conversation. I couldn't hear it and didn't think it would be appropriate to eavesdrop, not this time. What could be taking so long? The decision was easy. At least for me, it was. Tom didn't need to convince Bob that ghosts were real; Jimmy had done that. The only thing I could think of was Tom had to persuade him to help us solve this mystery.

The minutes passed; then I finally heard footsteps coming toward the door. The hinges creaked as the door opened, and Tom came outside wearing a huge smile. I couldn't wait to find out if he would help.

"Good night, Bob, and thanks for your help," Tom said.

Bob didn't say a word as he closed the door behind us.

"Sorry to keep you waiting."

"No problem. I understand," I replied.

"We'll swing by the store, throw your bike in the trunk of the car, and I'll give you a lift home."

"Oh, you don't have to do that."

"I insist; it's no trouble at all."

"Thank you for everything you've done for Jimmy and me." I wanted to get the conversation back on Jimmy and find out if Bob would help us. Okay, so I preferred to call him Old Man Smithers—Bob made it sound like we were friends, and we were far from being friends.

"I'm sure you want to know if Bob will help us locate Annabelle's remains." He looked at me and then turned his attention back to driving. "Bob said he would think about it. After all, it's a lot to take in for an adult."

"I get that." I remembered the first time I saw a ghost; I was speechless. Tom suddenly jammed on the brakes and swerved the car to the right, and we skidded off the road. My head jerked to the left, and my body felt twisted, but I wasn't hurt. Tom's eyes were wide, and he looked pale. "Are you okay, Tom?"

"Yes, are you?"

"I'm fine."

"Did you see the buck standing in the middle of the road?"

"No, I didn't see anything…"

"I think I drove through the deer but didn't feel any impact." Tom looked over his shoulder, and we noticed a large deer with a massive set of antlers next to the car, gazing in the window. Startled, we both jumped back. "What the heck!" he yelled. Tom grabbed the handle of the window and began to roll it down.

"What are you doing?" I warned. "This thing tried to kill us, and now you want to let him finish us off?"

Tom's eyes grew dark and appeared to roll back in his head. He turned to me. "What are you up to, boy?" he asked slowly in a voice I knew was not his.

"We're not up to anything. We're going home. That's all."

"Don't test my patience; tell me why you were at the house. What do you want with him?"

I realized I must be talking to Donald Thornhill. It had to be. Who else could it be? He was the only one that could transform into a deer and then take over a body. "What do you want, Mr. Thornhill?"

"You're a smart lad." It was weird talking to him and looking at Tom's face. "What do you want with my great-great-grandson?"

I was right; it was Donald Thornhill. I had a chance to ask my question right here and now, and I wasn't going to blow it. "We want to help." I must have caught him off guard because Tom's face pulled back. "We know how to cross you over; we want to help," I spit it out before he could leave.

"Why would I want to leave? I like it here, and I'm enjoying myself."

"We can send your spirit and Annabelle's to the other side. You could be together like you always wanted," I said.

He calmed himself, and his facial expression changed. "Why would you help me?" His voice was quiet, taking on a serious tone.

That was a great question, one that I needed to answer quickly. And it had better be a great response to convince Donald my offer was sincere. Then it hit me. "Doesn't everyone need help now and then?"

"I couldn't care less about you and your friends. I want to know what you're up to; I'm sure it's no good. Now, quit stalling and tell me!" he wailed.

"Mr. Thornhill, I'm trying to do the right thing. It was the way my father raised me, to help my fellow man. I know you're a ghost, but you still have feelings, and I truly want to help you and Annabelle."

"I don't believe you. It's a trick. I was fooled once in my life, and I won't let it happen again," he barked.

"Mr. Smithers buried Jacobs's body, and he crossed over. We can do the same for you and Annabelle," I begged.

"Yes, I whispered in my grandson's ear while he slept, and he did exactly what I told him to do. If you're not careful, I'll do the same to you," Donald said.

"I'm not afraid of you."

"Then you're a fool because I can make you do anything I want... I can even take your life."

A chill ran up my spine. This conversation was going nowhere. I knew I was wasting my time, but I couldn't give up. We needed to understand where Annabelle's body was buried if this plan would succeed. "Fine, don't tell us. I couldn't care less if you're stuck here forever. But if you told us, we could help you and Annabelle be together again."

"Heed my warning, boy—stop meddling in my affairs, or you'll pay the price." Tom's face turned angry. "Maybe I'll whisper something in your mother's ear…" he hissed.

"Don't threaten my family!" I yelled back.

"Why would I do that," Tom asked, dazed.

"Tom?"

"Who else would I be?"

"It's you. You're back." I smiled in relief. After I explained everything that had just happened, Tom was at a loss for words. He told me he was tired of spirits taking over his body, and I didn't blame him. I had no idea what that must be like, to lose your memory for a brief amount of time.

After waiting several minutes, we both felt it was time to move on. Tom backed the car onto the road, and we slowly drove to the store. I grabbed my bike from around the back and placed it inside the trunk. Tom said he was thirsty and ran inside to grab some milk.

We were back on the road in no time, and before I knew it, I was home. I lay in bed that night with the day's thoughts playing over in my head. I wish I had said some things differently, though I'm not sure it would have mattered.

After a restless night, it was back to school, our final week before summer vacation. It was more of a fun week with almost no homework. I always liked that—after all, it gave me more time to read the stories I enjoyed.

One day before lunch, I ran into Scooter and Todd in the hallway and brought them up to speed on the events of the weekend and our plans for this coming weekend. I also talked with Sara several times throughout the week, and she relayed my message to Lexi and Parker. And, of course, I had plenty of time to talk with Buck since we shared a house, not to mention a bedroom. It seemed like we were all on the same page, but one thing was still missing—was Tom able to convince Bob to help us locate the body? Once we had that information, we could proceed with our plans.

Everyone was eager for the week to end. Some of us had plans for the summer, and others would take things one day at a time. I planned to work and save as much money as possible as I had several good books I wanted to buy — one book, specifically, was Stephen King's newest book, *Salem's Lot*. He was a little-known author; his first book *Carrie* had come out over a year ago, and I loved that one, so I couldn't wait to get the new book and dig in. The title sounded right up my alley—witches and maybe even ghosts.

# EIGHTEEN

As the final bell rang, I bounced from my seat and headed to the bus, where I met Scooter. Instead of taking the bus, we decided to walk home. After all, we were teenagers and could do whatever we wanted now. We walked along Old Lizardville Road and kicked rocks along the way, oblivious to almost everything around us. We faintly heard the roar of water rushing over the dam; the sound grew louder as we approached. I hadn't walked out on the dam since we lost Jimmy. We stopped and looked at each other. With a slight nod, we decided it was time — that feeling that only close friends share.

We crossed the two-lane road and made our way over the guardrails and down the rocky embankment to the dam. It hadn't changed a bit. What remained of the dam was a ten-foot-wide walkway at the base, though it stood almost the same in height. The pitch of the dam made it easy to walk to the top, where it opened to another ten-foot-wide walkway. It stretched a hundred yards across the valley floor, reaching the base of the mountain. Big Fishing Creek flowed right up to it and then went to the south side, where the dam gave way when it broke some years ago. The water roared and swirled as it flowed around what remained of the broken concrete section.

The old control tower was located right in the middle of the dam. The structure stood some twenty feet in the air. Our old clubhouse's concrete room at the top had seen better days. I hadn't been up there in almost two years, and I'm sure the empty soda bottles we saved to return to the store and redeem our deposit money were no longer there. The view from the tower was amazing, and I missed looking out over the valley.

Standing a few feet short of the concrete walkway, I paused and took in the sights and sounds. It had been too long, and I was ready to conquer my fear. I even thought about running home to grab my fishing pole, but I knew we didn't have time. After a long pause, we each took a step forward, then another, and quickly felt the hard concrete under our feet. We walked out ten or twenty yards, and I paused to look out over the swirling water. Vividly, I remember the day Jimmy drowned. I had stood in this very spot, watching and waiting for him to surface. But he never did.

"Hey, Johnny, you alright?"

I turned to face Scooter. "Yeah, I'm fine." I pushed the words from my mouth. "I'm a little nervous being out here... you?"

"I get that. It brings back good and bad memories," Scooter said with a wry smile.

"It's time we close this chapter in our lives, and after this weekend, everything should be back to normal." If I could remember what normal was. Scooter nodded in agreement.

I felt we were on the same page—it would be nice not to see ghosts anymore.

Suddenly, a large crow flew into view and landed atop the overlook tower. I looked up and froze. I wasn't sure if we should run or stand our ground. I guess that depended on who the crow was. A second crow came into view; it circled for a minute and landed next to the larger one. Then another crow came, followed by another, and before we knew it, there must have been fifteen or twenty crows on the roof of the old tower. "Could they all be ghosts?" I whispered.

"It's not likely," Scooter said.

"Yeah, I suppose you're right."

Startled by the sound of shuffling feet behind us, I quickly turned to face the danger. Relief flooded my body when I saw Tom approach. "Hi, Mr. Evans, you startled me," I shouted.

"Oh, please, call me Tom. I've told you that. I don't know how many times."

"I was trying to be respectful in front of Scooter," I replied.

"Thank you, yet no need."

"What brings you out here?" I waved a hand around as if I was showing him the dam.

"Well, I saw you two out here and decided to tell you the good news," Tom said excitedly. "I spoke with Bob Smithers last night, and he knows where the body is supposed to be." Tom smiled.

"Really?" I had a sudden adrenaline rush. "That's far out!" I smiled at Tom and Scooter. "I can't wait to tell the others." I was getting a little ahead of myself.

"Slow down, big guy. First, we need to make sure the body is there, and if it is, how will we get it out and over to the cemetery without getting caught?" He looked at us with doubt in his eyes.

"Are you saying Old Man Smithers lied?" I asked.

"Why would Smithers lie?" Scooter asked.

"Good point," Tom interjected. "I don't think he lied. Maybe Bob didn't want to disappoint you, kids. Maybe he came up with this story to make you think he was helping. Or maybe he's telling the truth." Tom paused to let that sink in. "You may not know this, but he likes all of you."

"How about the fact that we are trying to help everyone," I smiled and shrugged off Tom's comment about Old Man Smithers liking us kids.

"I'm sure he's grateful for that, too. Something inside tells me not to believe him—maybe he could not convince his great-great-grandfather to tell him where he buried the body." Tom paused and rubbed his chin.

"What if he doesn't believe us and thinks we are all nut jobs or something like that? Hmmm?" Tom glanced at both of us.

"There's only one way to find out. Let's get the gang together and check it out." I smiled with an eager grin.

"I'm in," Scooter replied.

"I can't… at least, not right now. I must return to the store; I've been away longer than expected." Tom frowned. "But you guys could check it out."

"Right on." I smiled and looked at Scooter, who had this petrified look on his face. "Of course, we'll get the others to go with us when we go to the site," I said.

Scooter sighed. I knew what he was thinking, and I didn't blame him. I didn't want to go up the mountain with just us. Tom nodded as if he approved. All that was left was to know the location of the missing body, and then we could begin our quest.

"Good, that would make me feel better," Tom admitted.

One of the crows let out a loud warning caw. We all looked in the direction of the tower. Tom hadn't noticed them before, and he looked a bit nervous. "Are those all crows?" Tom asked. Scooter and I knew what he meant: *were they all ghosts?*

I raised my hands, and Scooter shrugged his shoulders to let him know that we didn't know for sure.

"Listen," he leaned forward, drawing closer to us, "Bob told me this…" He looked toward Parker's house on the other side of the road. We could tell that was the direction of the clue or the whereabouts of Annabelle's remains. "Take the path into the mountain—the same path that leads to the hidden cave—then follow that until it splits. It's about halfway up the mountain. When the path forks off, you go to the left. Stay on the lower path for a few hundred yards. Look for two trees that grew out of one trunk." He paused to look back at the crows on the top of the tower.

"When you find the tree, turn left and walk about fifty strides—a grown man's stride," he emphasized. "He said it would lead you to a small rock wall about ten or fifteen feet tall. The ground slopes around it, so it's easy to walk past it. Anyway, when you find the wall—" He glanced back at the tower, and so did I—the crows were getting restless. Some flew only a few feet from the tower, while others started flapping their wings and bouncing up and down. I had this bad feeling that something was about to happen.

"Don't walk past the rock wall. Smithers said if you get down on your hands and knees and look to the right side of the wall, you'll find a rock formation embedded in the wall that resembles a small cross. Bob said you need to dig at the base of the cross. She's buried a few feet down," he whispered to us.

"It doesn't make sense. Why wouldn't Robert Thornhill bury them in the same place?" I asked.

"If you think about it, it does make sense." Tom placed his hand on his chin for a moment. "According to history, Donald loved her. Why would he bury her with Jacob, the man she had feelings for?" Tom glanced back and forth between Scooter and me.

The squawking grew louder. The crows took flight, one after the other, circling the tower. A few broke off traveling to the north, some of the others flew to the south, and a couple flew over our heads. Much to our surprise, none of them posed any threat.

"I must be going." Tom motioned toward his car. "Let me know what you find out, and we can figure out our next move." He smiled and walked away.

Scooter and I agreed, and we took another look around the dam. I noticed one lonely crow sitting on the dam tower. Could that be Jimmy? Or worse, what if that was Annabelle, and she knew what we were up to?

"Let's head over to Parker's and see if anyone's home," I said. I crossed my arms, looked in that direction, and then looked back at the tower. "Can you give me a minute?"

"Sure, I'll wait by the road," Scooter said.

"Thanks." I smiled. I looked again at the tower and the lone crow perched at the top. I waited until Scooter was out of earshot. "Jimmy, if that's you… well, I want you to know one thing… This should all be over soon. I promise." Then I turned and looked at the swirling water that had claimed his life. "This is for you, buddy," I whispered as I slowly approached the road where Scooter waited.

Scooter was perched on the guardrails, resting his feet on the lower part. He cast a view my way. "You good?"

"Yeah, I'm good." I smiled.

He hopped off the rail, and we strolled across the road, onto Parker's lawn, and up the sidewalk. I knocked on the door and waited. The door opened to the sight of Sara. She smiled when she saw it was me. "Hi."

I smiled back, and she stepped aside to let us in. "Is Parker home?"

"Everyone's here, kind of the last day of school gathering if you know what I mean."

She turned, and we followed her down to the basement.

"Hey," a few shouted, and the others waved as Scooter and I came down the stairs. The whole gang was here. Buck, Parker, Todd, and Lexi were chatting in the corner. Sara led us over as the room fell silent.

"Where you been, dude?" Buck asked. "We didn't see you on the bus."

"Scooter and I decided to walk." I glanced back.

"Tell 'em the news." Scooter tugged at my arm.

"Why don't you?" I shot back.

I think Scooter lost his voice after that because he remained silent. He motioned with his head, pointing at the others, the excitement killing him.

"Alright, alright. We ran into Tom at the dam." Everyone froze and looked at us as if they didn't believe us. "Yes, we went out on the dam. It's been long enough, and we decided to get past our fear today. Anyway, Tom said he talked with Old Man Smithers and found out the location where,"

I dragged the words out to build the suspense, then whispered, "her body's buried."

"So, he told you?" Buck replied.

"Yes, yes, he did." I smiled. "And it's not too far from here."

"What are we waiting for?" Lexi chimed in as she pulled on Buck's arm.

"So, what's the plan? Find the body? Dig it up? Then what? And what if Annabelle shows up, huh?" I'm not ashamed to admit that I was afraid. *We were dealing with powers that were beyond our control. What would happen if she felt threatened? Who knew what Annabelle could do? I'd seen Jimmy do things; he'd only been a ghost for two years. Annabelle had been around for eighty years.*

"Don't be a pansy," Buck said. Todd, Parker, and Lexi agreed—they wanted to go now.

I was shocked when Scooter piped in with a grimace, "Can we get this over with, please?"

"Okay then, let's go," I said hesitantly. Sara touched my arm and gave me a cute little smile. Parker and Buck shuttled around, grabbing two shovels, an old blanket, and a few other things we may end up needing. Lexi filled two canteens and passed them to Todd to carry. Finally, the seven of us went to the basement door leading to the backyard.

# NINETEEN

**W**e nudged the door open and started across the lawn, making our way to the woods. We'd hiked this trail a dozen times, so it was no mystery to us where the path would lead. Parker, Todd, Buck, and Lexi led the way, followed by Scooter and me.

We continued our ascent up the mountain. It was about thirty minutes before we came to the location where the path split in two directions. We forked off to the left, taking the lower path. The other direction would send us farther up the mountain, toward the cave, while this direction stayed more on an even level with the mountain, not going up or down. We trudged along, and in no time at all, we spotted the two trees that grew from the same trunk. It's funny how you always hike these woods, but you never notice something like this tree. I guess Mr. Thornhill had a keen eye and paid attention to detail. Once we knew it was there, it stood out like a sore thumb.

We paused for a minute to catch our breath. Lexi passed around the canteen. I said no to the water, and so did some of the others. I guess we were saving our swigs of water for when the digging would start. We pushed off, one by one, stepping into the freshly grown foliage. It's a good thing it was early summer and not the middle or even the end of summer—the vegetation would be a lot thicker than it was. Parker picked up a long branch and snapped a few smaller branches off, trimming the stick to his needs. Swinging the large branch from side to side flattened out some of the weeds and made a path for us to mark our way back to the trail, and it also made it a little easier on our journey. I could hear him counting paces as he walked. Our excitement level was increasing with every step. I noticed a rock wall that was protruding out of the ground. It reached ten to twelve feet in height and stretched about twenty-five or thirty feet in length before it sloped upward and faded into the landscape.

I looked around, focusing on the lush, dense cover of the trees. I felt better knowing it was thick and should provide coverage from an overhead attack. I couldn't even see the blue sky. I didn't see how any crow could fly over and spot us down here. Then I wondered if a ghost had a different sense I didn't know about. *I guess that is something I should ask Jimmy the next time I see him.*

I turned my attention back to the wall. I'm not sure how anyone would ever realize this was a gravesite. Buck, Parker, and Todd were already looking along the wall for a rock formation that looked like a cross. They moved their hands along its surface, scouring every inch of the wall. I watched from a distance, as did Scooter and Sara, listening for any sounds of trouble.

"I think I found something," Lexi screeched. We could see the excitement in her expression. "Hurry, come look at this!" She ran her fingers across a small formation about a foot off the ground. After the older boys took their turns, I squeezed in and confirmed it was a cross shape.

My eyes bulged as I gazed upon the small cross embedded in the wall. It's funny how nature works. There was a ten-inch cross, as plain as day and almost perfectly arranged in the stones. I quickly snapped out of it when Buck thrust a shovel into my hands.

"Start digging," he demanded.

"Why me?" I grabbed the shovel in a quick, even motion.

"Because I said so." Buck rammed another shovel at Scooter.

I looked around and saw that the older boys and Lexi had taken seats on a fallen tree that stretched across the forest floor. Sara was quick to join them. I turned back to face the wall and looked over at Scooter, who was staring at me. "I guess we dig here." I pointed at the spot below the marking on the wall and sunk my shovel into the hard ground. Scooter snickered as I saw that my shovel had only gone in about two inches. I smiled and shook my head, knowing this would be a long afternoon.

The digging continued for almost an hour. I couldn't help but wonder how special this spot must have been to Donald Thornhill. Did he and Annabelle have quiet little picnics here? Was this their favorite spot? Sweat dripped from my forehead. I glanced at the two-, maybe three-foot hole in the ground. I needed a break. Parker and Buck pulled the shovels from our hands and told us to take five. I took a few swigs of water, and before I could finish my last gulp, Buck jammed the shovel back into my hands. I was a little upset but didn't say anything as I climbed back into the hole and plunged the shovel into the dirt. The deeper

we went, the easier the digging became as the ground soft-
ened. I was stunned that we found no large rocks as we dug.
I guess I thought this would be rocky. Being so close to a
rock wall meant we must be in the right spot. We did hit a
few tree roots as we continued our descent, but nothing we
couldn't manage.

Another hour passed, and we were down another foot or
two. The hole was getting wider as well. I thought we would
have found something by now. We were both exhausted,
hands hurting; I looked at the blisters on the palms of my
hands. I dug slower—it was so hard to keep going. I wondered if there was something that Tom had forgotten to tell
us, or maybe Old Man Smithers had failed to tell Tom all
the clues, or perhaps this was just some wild goose chase.
I had tossed my shovel out of the hole and started to climb
out when Scooter hit something.

Excited, I turned around to see what he'd struck. Then
we heard strange sounds coming from the woods. I was
afraid that Annabelle was going to stop us. It was a loud
screeching sound, but it sounded more like a man's voice
than a woman's. I looked back at the hole and noticed
Scooter was slowly moving dirt with his hand to the blade
of the shovel and tossing it out of the hole. I shot a look
down the path we had made through the woods and noticed
the figure of a man—to my surprise, it was Tom. I thought
he had to go back to the store. After all, this was the last
day of school and one of his busiest days. It proved to
me that Tom cared more about us kids than he would like
us to think.

Behind Tom was an older woman, someone I had never
seen before. She was old and wrinkly and had frizzy white
hair that cascaded halfway down her back. I would have

thought Tom had brought a witch if I didn't know better. She wore a long heavy black dress with thick black shoes that came up to her ankles. Her glasses were thick. Maybe she was blind? She was carrying a device with smoke pouring out of it that swung on a chain. It reminded me of something an altar boy or priest would carry down the center of the aisle at church. Maybe this one was filled with incense, too. I could smell this funny odor all the way down the path.

"Hi." Tom and the woman stopped and caught their breath. "This is my mother, Gladys Evans," he said. She stayed focused on what she was doing as she mumbled words to herself. She walked in a circle around us. "She's warding off evil spirits. It's a protection chant to keep us safe. The chamber is filled with white sage. Ghosts can't stand the smell." He smiled.

"What are you doing here?" I asked.

He looked surprised. "I thought you would be happy to see me."

"I am," I said, and from the looks of the others, so were they.

"I know you guys well enough to know that you would dig up the site today, and I couldn't let you do that on your own." Tom cocked his head and gave me a wry smile.

I watched the old woman as she walked around and mumbled to herself. I felt someone tug on my sleeve. "Hey, are you going to help?" Scooter asked.

I turned my attention back to the hole in the ground. Scooter had made some real progress. I noticed something. I dropped to my knees and used my hands to push the dirt to the side. It was an old blanket or carpet, which could only mean one thing. We had found her remains. "I think we found it!" I shouted, looking at the others who peered at us from the top of the hole. I was elated. We could now help Jimmy cross over; there was nothing more I wanted to do than help my friend.

"Hurry, we need to get her out of there," Lexi demanded.

I crawled out as Buck, Parker, and Todd relieved Scooter and me from our duties. The minute we were out, Tom handed each of us a rock. I looked puzzled, but only momentarily—I felt I knew what these stones were. "It's a rose quartz stone. It helps to dissolve negative vibes and replace them with positive ones," Tom clarified.

"What?" Scooter asked, looking puzzled.

"Haven't you been paying attention?" I asked. "It helps to keep away ghosts and helps them to keep an open and positive mind if they do come."

"Oh, well, that makes sense." Scooter looked around, trying to figure out where to put the stone before he jammed it into his pocket.

"I have a red wagon back on the path," *Tom had thought of everything—protection for all of us and a way to carry her back to the car. Now I knew why we needed him involved.* "If we can carry the package to the path, we should be able to wheel it down the rest of the way to the car," Tom said.

Rustling sounds came from the branches above. Sara and Lexi screamed, and I spotted two large crows bouncing from branch to branch. They appeared to be fighting. I thought one must be Annabelle, and the other was probably Donald Thornhill… or were they just two birds playing in the woods? They didn't swoop down at us or even attempt to. Maybe the white sage Tom's mother was burning kept them at bay. I glanced over at the dig site. The older boys were making significant progress.

"I'll be right back," Tom yelled before darting through the woods. *I thought he was getting scared and running, but why would he leave his mother behind?* She continued to chant and walk in circles around all of us. The old lady looked to be in a daze, and I wasn't exactly sure she knew where she was.

Scooter and Sara looked nervous as the crows came closer and closer toward us. I looked for any loose stones lying around, and I found several. Quickly, I grabbed one and tossed it in the direction of the birds. Scooter was quick to follow my lead. The loud thudding sound of footsteps approached. Tom had returned and was carrying a large green duffle bag—the style of bag our men and women in the military used.

He tossed the bag next to the hole. "Put the remains in here. It will be easier to carry that way," he barked. The squawking sound of the crows had begun to fade—they must not have liked the stones we were hurling in their direction.

"Give me the bag!" Parker yelled. Sara bent over and pushed the sack into the hole. As we glanced down, I watched the boys inch the dried-up blanket with something wrapped inside it into the large canvas bag. My excitement level had peaked. I couldn't wait to get this thing out of here and to the cemetery. The sooner this was all over, the better.

The crows calmed down and remained perched in the trees above. The temperature remained the same, which was also a good sign. "Johnny? Guys? Grab the bag!" Buck yelled.

I turned toward the top of the hole and noticed the green bag approaching me. I stretched out my hand, latched onto the handle, and tugged with all my might. Scooter and Tom quickly joined me, and in a matter of seconds, the bag was resting at our feet. I watched Tom zip up the bag, but not before I caught a glimpse of some human bones, and I shivered. I turned and extended a hand to Parker, then Buck, and helped to pull them from the pit. Todd was the only one who didn't need help. In one giant leap, he bounced out on his own.

Tom signaled for his mother to lead the way. She turned toward the tall grass that would lead us to the trail and get us home. I grabbed a corner of the bag, and the older boys each took a corner. We quietly made our way, following Mama Evans, Tom, Sara, and Lexi, with Scooter and us boys bringing up the rear. We all kept a sharp eye out for any unusual movement. I think we all knew we were not out of danger yet. I had this eerie feeling our troubles were only beginning.

The weeds thinned out, and I spotted the girls stepping onto the trail and turning right as they walked down the slope. Tom didn't lie—he had brought a red metal wagon with him, and it was parked next to the path. We gently placed the bag in the back, and I watched Tom grab the handle and pull it. The rest of us fell in behind him.

The smell of the white sage had begun to make my nose itch. It twitched from side to side as if I had to sneeze, yet I never did. Scooter had a tear in his eye and had mentioned it was making his eyes water. However, we both knew a few irritations were better than fighting a ghost or two. We continued downward, and Parker's house came into view in no time. We stopped and assessed the situation. We were fifty or sixty yards from the house with nothing but open yard and no overhead protection.

We lingered behind a minute and waited for the girls to make it to the house. Lexi made sure no one was home. We had caught a break because Parker's parents were in town having a few drinks with friends and wouldn't be back until late. She waved us forward. Tom's mother started first, trailed by a cloud of smoke. Then Tom pulled the wagon and broke into the clearing. The older boys flanked Tom on each side as they looked toward the trees. The coast was still free of any danger. I held my breath, and then Scooter poked me in the side and pointed to the edge of the clearing. I noticed a large gathering of crows on the far-left side scattered throughout the trees. I think this was the first time I realized it was getting late in the day, and the sun would soon go down.

The wagon train made its way slowly across the yard. Twenty yards, then fifteen… we were so close; I could smell victory. Lexi pushed the basement door open, and Tom pulled the wagon inside. *Right on*, I thought. *Everything was going as planned*. In fact, it was going better than I expected.

# TWENTY

It wasn't time to celebrate, not yet anyway. We needed to get the remains to the cemetery and lay them to rest. But first, we had one other thing to do. One by one, we went upstairs to use the phone. Buck phoned home and told our parents we were staying at Parker's house for the night, and Scooter and Todd did the same. Lexi left a note that she and Sara were staying at her friend Lisa's and that Parker would stay at our house for the night. Now that we had that out of the way, it was time to go to the cemetery.

"Hold up," Tom said something to Parker just out of earshot, and they went upstairs. In the blink of an eye, they returned. "There was no answer," Tom said.

I was puzzled, and by the looks of the others, so were they. "Tom called Old Man Smithers," Parker said, "but he wasn't home." He frowned.

"Yes, he's either at the cemetery waiting on us or on his way," Tom added.

"Not to cast doubt, but we have no clue where he is, do we?" Todd asked. Quite frankly, I had to agree with Todd on this one. We could arrive and find him at the cemetery, or we could have to dig another grave by ourselves. I was hoping for the first.

"I guess we'll find out when we get there," Parker barked as he motioned toward the door.

"I'll go across the road and back my car up as close to the back door as possible," Tom announced. "The rest of you will have to ride with Lexi."

I was glad Lexi had bought a used car a few months ago—it made it easier for all of us to get around. It was a 1971 Ford Pinto, yellow with a black roof. It reminded me of a bumble bee, but I wouldn't bring that up in front of Lexi. The car was only five years old and ran well, but it was small, so we had difficulty fitting five people inside. Sara sat up front with her sister while Todd, Scooter, and I were crammed in the back seat.

I watched as Buck, Parker, and Tom loaded the large green duffle bag into the back of Tom's car, his mother sitting in the front still chanting. They closed the trunk and hopped in. I chuckled as I watched smoke pour out of all the windows when they pulled away from the driveway.

Lexi followed close behind. I guess that was in case something were to happen. Personally, I felt safer riding in the second car. Sara turned to look at me a few times, stilling me with her smile. We drove past our house on the right-hand side of the road. I noticed Dad washing his car in the front yard as we passed.

My mind flashed back to the day Jimmy died. We had walked down Lizardville Road, the same route we took today. As we drove by the motorcycle shop, I thought of the Styrofoam crates we used to take from the back of the shop. We turned them into makeshift rafts so we could float down Big Fishing Creek. I think Scooter was doing the same thing I was because I noticed his head was bobbing a little, and he had a wry smile on his face.

Lexi drove up a small hill and then down, past the lumber yard. Jimmy used to live next door, and the guys who worked at the mill thought Jimmy played tricks on them. They never cared for him, yet they all attended his funeral. I remember the day the workers chased us, thinking we were up to no good. I smiled. I had plenty of good memories, thinking about all the times we played hide and seek at the sawmill.

Lexi drove a little farther down a long straightaway. Big Fishing Creek appeared, and I could see the boulders that lined the walls of the stone quarry on the left-hand side. Parker used to hang out there when he was younger. I was not sure how much time he spent there these days. It was his place to go and think and dream of being a space cadet. One of the giant pits had filled up with water, and from time to time we would go there to swim—even after our parents had told us it was too deep; we shouldn't swim there. Now, there's a chain link fence around the crater to keep us kids out, and it's plastered with no trespassing signs.

She continued to drive as the first bridge came into view. Sitting on the left side of the bridge was Tom's general store. I flashed back to the day Jimmy passed away. I had a close call with Tom and Old Man Smithers in the store that day, and all that money was in lovely little stacks piled on the top of Tom's desk. I was glad I did the right thing and didn't steal any of it. After all, in time, Tom had asked me to work for him, and he'd become a pretty good friend.

The next bridge came into view, and I thought about all the times we used to jump off the bridge and swim. I remember when Parker was being a butt and forced Scooter to jump, all because Scooter was scared. I remembered how brave Jimmy was. Even though he was being held down at the bottom of the water by Annabelle, he still came back to the top and jumped off the bridge again. The boy had no fear, or was it that he didn't think any harm could come to him? Yes, it can happen to anyone, even me, and in Jimmy's case, it did. Too many of us today don't realize how precious life is.

As we rounded a long right-hand curve in the road, we could see Old Man Smithers' house to our left. The bluffs on the far side overlooked the creek and all that property for one lonely old man. I couldn't stop thinking about how often he chased us and yelled that we were trespassing on his land when we floated past his house. Yet today, we would be working with him at the cemetery. I didn't notice his car parked out front—which was a good sign. Tom must have been correct when he said Bob would be waiting for us at the cemetery.

We sat in silence as Lexi continued our drive down Lizardville Road. Today could be the final chapter in this story. Annabelle and Thornhill should be laid to rest, and with some luck, that would resolve their issues and cross them over. I pursed my lips to suppress the smile. The victory was within reach. Only a few things remained—locate Jimmy's body, say goodbye, and lay him to rest. That was the plan; we all knew how well my plans worked out. Okay, sometimes they went according to plan. This evening I felt confident.

The car slowed, and I looked to my right. I could see the black wrought iron gates to Lizardville Cemetery come into view. I looked to Scooter and then to Sara—both had the same petrified look on their face. Seeing such a look on Sara's face was excruciating, but what was I to do? I felt scared and helpless too. We were dealing with powers we didn't fully understand, and anything could go wrong.

The brakes screeched, and the car pulled to a stop. Lexi parked close to Tom, and I could see the older boys were already leaving the vehicle. I glanced around and didn't see Old Man Smithers' car. My heart was pounding, and I thought it would leap out of my chest. I noticed Tom wave before the boys got back in the car. Lexi put the car back in drive and followed Tom's car through the grass. Lexi stayed close behind Tom as she drove her car through the tall weeds and made her way along the fence to the back of the cemetery. I'd never been back here before—it must have been the old ghost stories that had kept most of us away from this place. Once again, the brakes screeched, and the car stopped. This time Lexi turned the keys and shut the car off. It was quiet, almost too quiet for me. The older boys were getting out of Tom's car, and so was the old lady carrying her plume of smoke. We hesitated to leave the car; no one wanted to be first. Okay, maybe we were just too scared to get out.

Todd, who had remained hushed on the way here, opened the door. My heart jumped in my chest. I was not sure I had ever been that scared in my life. I had this uneasy feeling that something was about to happen, especially since everything had gone as planned up to this point. I pulled the handle and opened my side of the car, placing a foot outside in the tall grass. The cool evening air smacked me in the face. I hadn't noticed before how dark it was getting. Maybe it was because we were in the back of the cemetery and there were no streetlights.

I glanced around and saw rows and rows of tombstones. Some were large, others small, some leaning forward, while the taller ones leaned back. How many graves were in the cemetery was mind-boggling—something I never paid much attention to. Lexi, Sara, and Scooter all stepped out to join Todd and me. I looked at Buck, Parker, Tom, and the old lady. Out of the corner of my eye, I spotted Old Man Smithers approaching. There were ten of us in all. With this many people, I felt a little more secure. They say there is strength in numbers, and we had the numbers. But that could be easily outmatched by otherworldly powers.

"I don't know if I could do what you guys did," Daniel interrupted.

"Sure, we could. I'm not afraid of anything," Zack yelled as he pushed out his chest.

The boys had been reticent up to this point. "I make it sound easy, but in all honesty, I was scared out of my wits," I admitted. "Look, I don't advise doing any of this if you can help it. But we faced something strange that summer and needed to correct it. This was the only option we had." I frowned.

"So, what happened next?" Daniel asked as he sank back into his chair.

Old Man Smithers and Tom shook hands. "Glad you could make it," Tom said.

"Thank you for asking. Now, can we get this over with?" Bob smirked.

"I agree. I don't like this place and don't want to be here at night," Tom replied.

I was in total agreement with Tom. I didn't want to be here, either. But I was standing in the back of Lizardville Cemetery looking at all the grave markers. Who knew how many ghosts roamed this place? The hairs on my arms stood up. I spotted a few bats taking flight from the trees. The lightning bugs flickered in and out in the surrounding fields. The crickets chirped, and nightfall was upon us. I watched as Bob Smithers pointed to an enormous headstone. We walked in that direction until the stone was before us. The name on the right side of the stone shocked me. *Donald Thornhill is a loving husband, father, and business owner. 1858-1904*. Wow, he was only forty-six. He looked much older than that when I'd seen him.

Another name was carved in the middle of the large rock: *Annabelle Thornhill, a loving wife and mother. 1879-1904*. It struck me that she was only twenty-five. I knew her remains were not in this spot that bore her name. Much to my surprise, a third name on the left side was *Elizabeth Thornhill, loving daughter, 1900-1972*. I stood in silence as did the others. My jaw dropped open—she had been alive in recent years, and I had no idea. I don't think any of us had realized that. She was most likely the last person to be laid to rest in this cemetery.

That's when I noticed the gaping hole that Bob Smithers had dug in front of the Thornhills' headstone. The hole was deep, maybe five or six feet. He had carefully removed the top layer with the grass still intact. It would be easier to place the pieces back on top giving the appearance that no one had ever tampered with the site. All we had to do was put the remains of Annabelle into the hole and cover her up. It sounded simple, maybe too simple. Donald would be at peace because his wife had returned to where she belonged. Annabelle would be beside her husband and daughter, and with any luck, they would both cross over; then, we could work on helping Jimmy. It was almost too easy.

# TWENTY-ONE

A loud commotion erupted in the trees to our left as a chilling blast of wind raced across the field. I cursed under my breath. I knew things were going too smoothly. Annabelle burst out of the trees with a roar. Her high-pitched screams rattled our senses. We dropped to our knees and covered our ears to muffle the sound. Quickly, another translucent figure bolted from the woods—Donald Thornhill. He pointed in her direction, and I spotted a light beam shoot from his finger directly at Annabelle. I couldn't believe what I was witnessing. Annabelle spun around and waved her hand and deflected his shot. With a swipe of her hand, a large beam of light flashed across the field, hitting Donald and sending him tumbling back to the tree line.

The screaming stopped. I turned to find Sara frozen in place a few steps away. I darted over, quickly grabbed her, and pulled her behind a large tombstone to shield us from the fight that was taking place before our eyes. I noticed many of the others had taken cover, too. The only one who remained was Tom's mother. She stood next to the open grave site; she was chanting and waving the canister from side to side. She didn't appear to be afraid at all. Maybe it was the stones that protected her, or perhaps the smell the smoke was putting off as it continued to pour out of the canister made her feel safe in the middle of the ghostly fight.

I gripped the edge of the headstone and peered over the top—a flash of light to the right, another shot back to the left. Two blurry incandescent light figures were fighting before my eyes, both determined to defeat the other. Swish and a whoosh, they beamed around in a blur. The action looked like something you would see in a Hollywood movie.

I spotted Old Man Smithers dart from behind the tombstone and dash toward Tom's car. Tom stood up and followed close behind. I felt helpless. The battle moved closer in the direction of the cars. Annabelle paused and then made a beeline for Tom. In a flash, she was standing beside Tom and Bob. She screamed, and both of them collapsed to their knees and covered their ears. I don't know why or what I was thinking, but I stood and walked in the direction of the car. The stones in my pocket would protect me; I was sure of it.

I ducked behind the last gravestone at the edge of the cemetery. Tom and Bob were still on their knees as Annabelle continued her raging. She stood firm, one hand to her side and the other stretched out, pointing at Donald, who appeared to be held in the same location. *How long could a person—okay, so she's not technically a person— well, how long could a ghost scream?* I wondered. I'm unsure when, but I noticed a few stones beside the grave marker. I bent over, picked them up, and tossed the first one at Annabelle. A perfect shot passed straight through her, and I must have caught her by surprise because she stopped screaming, and her outstretched hand fell to her side as she turned her head in my direction.

*Oh no, what have I done?* I ducked behind the headstone, hoping she would not come after me. I stayed low to the ground and peeked around the edge. I noticed Tom and Bob had uncovered their ears. I watched as Bob bounced to his feet and opened the trunk of the car, Tom right at his side. I was fixated on Bob and Tom, watching as they started to pull the duffle bag from the car. I stood up to get a better look. I didn't notice that Annabelle was waving her hand in my direction. I spotted a bright flash of light out of the corner of my eye, and it hit me like a locomotive. I felt the sting in my chest and the oxygen squeeze from my lungs. I must have been launched several feet in the air because I hit the ground with such force that it knocked the wind out of me. I watched little stars float in a circle above my head. I didn't think a ghost could harm a human. I guess I was wrong about that, just like I was wrong about the stones in my pocket. They were supposed to protect me, but they didn't. I lay there looking upward at the dark evening sky. The stars looked amazing. I wondered what it would be like to travel through space. I flashed back to my childhood days, brief flashes of one event after another. *Am I dying? Will I be a ghost like Jimmy?* I couldn't bear the thought of leaving my brother and parents behind, not to mention Sara. I don't know how long I was on my back as time seemed to slow. In the distance, I heard Sara and Lexi scream, the last thing I remembered before passing out.

"Are you alright?"

"Johnny? Johnny?"

Someone shook me. "Johnny, wake up."

They shook me again, harder this time. "Dude, wake up," Buck shouted.

I could hear the words but only felt the pain in my chest and watched as lights flickered in and out. The screaming continued, and I opened my eyes and noticed Buck's panicked look. A crooked smile appeared when he knew I was alright. I think I even saw a tear trickle down the side of his cheek.

"You dork." He punched me in the arm. "You scared me." He smiled and laughed.

I smiled back, took a deep breath, and tried to regain my faculties. I placed my hand on my chest to see if there was a hole in me. There wasn't, and I breathed a sigh of relief. Buck grabbed my hand and pulled me to a sitting position. My throat was dry, and my stomach felt empty. I looked around as the battle raged on.

Annabelle had more power than any of us could have imagined. I think she was even stronger than Donald Thornhill. Or was Donald holding back because he loved her so much? *That had to be it*. Of course, I'm not sure a ghost can feel pain or even get hurt like we humans can. I knew that wouldn't help any of us today, but I'd have to remember to ask Jimmy when I saw him.

I looked across the field. Bob and Tom were hunched over with one knee on the ground and the green duffle bag lying between them. They were making progress as they inched their way toward the open grave. If we could only distract Annabelle long enough to give them the time they needed to make it the rest of the way, this could all be over. I shared my plan with Buck, who motioned to Todd and Parker. They both made a mad dash in our direction, and then Buck whispered the plan to the others.

Parker held up his hand and counted with his fingers. We would all start at the same time. *One, two, three!* Parker lunged to his feet and bolted to the right about twenty feet, then turned and ran straight for Annabelle. Todd bounced up and ran some twenty feet to the left before turning and running toward Annabelle. Buck and I leaped to our feet and ran directly at Annabelle, about five feet between us. We sprinted, trying to reach her at the same time. I wasn't sure what to do when we arrived, but I guess we would figure it out together. How do you tackle a ghost? But that was the only plan we could devise, so it had better work. You could tell we were desperate, though I think it was more of a distraction than anything. This would allow Tom and Bob the time they needed to get her remains to the empty hole we hoped would be her new home. Scooter stood up from the tombstone he was hiding behind and tossed a rock at Annabelle; then, he ducked back down to take cover. I wish I had thought of throwing and ducking before I got knocked flat on my back. I sprinted toward Annabelle, as did the others. We all kept our heads down. Parker was the first to arrive and dove right at her. With the wave of a hand, he was tossed to the side like a sack of potatoes.

Bob and Tom slipped to their feet, grabbed the bag, and started toward the open grave. Todd was the next to arrive, and he passed right through Annabelle on his way to the ground. It appeared to take some of the steam out of her as she spun around to look at him. Todd turned over to his back and looked directly at her, and I could see the fear written all over his face. Buck lunged forward to grapple with Annabelle, but like the others, he fell face-first in the dirt before scurrying to his back to face her.

I screamed with anger and lunged at her with total momentum. She spun and looked at me as if I could somehow harm her. I guess that was a human or ghostly instinct that kicked in, the response when facing your attacker. I fell to the ground like the others. She appeared upset to think we could even come close to matching her strength. It was preposterous to believe we could have fazed her, but our plan worked. Out of the corner of my eye, I noticed Tom and Bob were only a few yards away from victory. I cocked an eyebrow and watched with excitement.

Annabelle raised both her arms and thrust them forward with a brilliant spark of light. The bag dropped as Tom and Bob were launched into the air, knocking them a few feet away. I gritted my teeth—I could feel their pain from here. Donald Thornhill floated over the bag and cast his sight downward. A sad reflection of a once-proud man and factory owner, he clearly loved and cared for his wife. The rejection he was feeling was evident by the look on his face.

Annabelle was winning the battle. She knew what we were trying to accomplish. There wasn't much we could do to stop her. She rocketed to the bag and was about to move it away from the grave when a giant flash of light appeared. Stunned and panicked, she recoiled as the light made its way in her direction.

Shaken and out of breath, I watched helplessly from behind the safety of a headstone as Jimmy bolted onto the scene. He went directly for Annabelle and passed through her in one swift move. She spiraled to the ground and appeared to be unconscious. Once again, Jimmy had waited for the perfect time to arrive.

"Move!" Tom yelled.

He and Bob scrambled to their feet, and each grabbed a strap on the bag, picked it up, and swung it swiftly. The bag lunged toward the open grave. Bullseye! I watched as the bag tumbled out of sight. Bob smiled and reached for the shovel, but before he could pour the first load of dirt, the shovel was dislodged from his hand by a ray of light.

Annabelle looked petrified, and I watched as she bolted sparks at Tom and Bob. They both crawled on their hands and knees to the nearest gravestone and took cover. Tom was kicking dirt in the direction of the hole, trying to start the process of filling the grave as he moved away. Gladys looked on as she continued her chant and waved the smoke-filled canister from side to side. I still was not sure if that was doing any good. However, Annabelle never tried to harm her.

I knew we had to do something. There were too many of us to let Annabelle win. We had to send her to the other side and end this right here and now. I jumped to my feet, unsure what I would do or say. I started walking in the direction of the open grave.

"No, what are you doing?" Sara screamed as she stood to watch me. Lexi tried to pull her down with little luck.

Todd, Buck, and Parker rolled forward as the four of us scurried toward the mound of dirt needed to fill the hole. Tom's mom hovered around the open grave. Tom and Bob regained their balance as they scrambled to their feet. Before Annabelle could strike, Jimmy tossed a fireball at her. The impact rocked her back on her heels. Donald approached from her blindside and tackled her to the ground.

I was amazed. I didn't know one ghost could grab another spirit and hold them down. Jimmy spun his hands around in a circle and whipped up a pale-colored rope as he approached Annabelle. The rest of us hurried toward the dirt pile and did everything we could to fill the hole quickly. We used our hands and feet to push the dirt into the open pit. The sound of earth hitting the canvas sack quickly turned to softer thuds as it landed on top of more soil. Bob and Tom used the shovels as dirt flowed into the giant crater. Bit by bit, the hole started to fill up.

I turned my head and watched the old lady walk in a circle around Donald, Jimmy, and Annabelle, surrounding them with smoke and trapping them inside. Annabelle squirmed and kicked, trying to break free, but this time she was overpowered. She let out one more of her loud screams that brought us all to our knees, but that quickly subsided, and we continued to launch dirt into the hole. Annabelle's voice sounded raspy. Her translucent figure started to dissipate. She blinked in and out for a second or two, and her voice faded. Something was happening. We were winning.

"Stop, please stop… Gladys, you're my great-granddaughter. How could you do this to your family, to me? Please," she begged.

We continued to pile more dirt into the hole. I watched as the soil grew closer to the top. Jimmy took a few steps back, as did her husband. She frowned, a tear tracing down her face. Donald smiled. They were both getting lighter. I grappled with what was happening. Our plan was working—she would cross over and be gone.

Annabelle struggled to stand, casting a look in our direction. "Why…?" Her entire body blinked in and out, and her eyes drooped in defeat. Her face was animated with a look of shock and disgust as tears rolled down her cheeks. "Why?" she mouthed. "Why?" Then, she vanished.

Donald Thornhill stood triumphantly. He hovered off the ground a few feet, taking his place over his grave marker. He bowed toward us and smiled—something he hadn't done in some time, I'm sure. Casting a look at each of us, he mouthed, "Thank you," before he faded into the ground and moved to another world.

My mouth fell open. I glanced around, and all of us were doing the same. We were all in awe of what had transpired in the cemetery. Tom's mother closed the doors on the side of the canister, and the smoke stopped polluting the air. Tom and Bob smiled, hugged each other, and then shook hands. Scooter finally reappeared from his hiding spot and looked at the rest of us. I smiled back.

I quickly thought about Jimmy and looked from one side of the graveyard to the other, but he was nowhere in sight. Bob and Tom finished placing the grass pieces on the top of the mound of dirt to finish off Annabelle's grave. None of us were sure what would happen next.

"Dude, that was awesome," Zack exclaimed.

"Did that really happen?" Daniel asked with a wry smile.

"I know you may not believe it, but yes, all this happened." I paused and licked my lips. I didn't realize I had been talking for hours. I stood up and walked to the kitchen to grab a glass of water. "Would you like something to drink?" I shouted back to the family room.

"No, I'm good," they said in unison.

I filled up the glass with water from the refrigerator door and made my way back to the chair. "Boys, I don't expect you to understand, but that was a night I wish I could

forget. I wore a brave face that day, yet inside, I was petrified. More than I had ever been." I sank back in the chair
and took a long sip of the water.

"Is there more?" Daniel asked.

"What happened to Jimmy?" Zack questioned.

I smiled at my boys and continued my story.

# TWENTY-TWO

Joyous, we jumped up and down in celebration. Buck, Parker, and Todd slapped each other's hands and yelled, "Did you see that? Did you see me? Oh, did you see what I did?" Each one was trying to act like their role was more important than the others.

Sara lunged at me and wrapped her arms around my neck. The force almost knocked me to the ground.

"You scared me." She pouted. Her eyes were watery.

"I'm sorry." I didn't know what else to say as I stood there enjoying the prolonged hug. For the first time in days, I felt as if a weight had been lifted off my shoulders. I couldn't believe our plan actually worked and that this was finally over. Annabelle and Donald Thornhill were gone, I hoped.

"Nice job." Tom patted me on the back as he walked toward his car with Gladys trailing behind. She never spoke directly to any of us, which I thought was a bit odd. No wonder Tom never talked about his mother.

Even Bob Smithers patted us all on the backs as he made his way to his car from the back of the cemetery. I spotted Lexi and Buck holding hands as they got into her car. "Wait, who am I riding with?" I yelled. Standing next to his car, Tom waved and motioned for me to join him. Sara, Scooter, and I decided to join Tom and his mom. I stopped short of Tom's car, watching Scooter and Sara crawl into the back seat.

I turned and looked around the graveyard. Things were quiet now. It was hard to believe there had been a ghostly battle here only a few moments ago. Jimmy got what he wanted. All that remained was to break his curse, and I knew what I needed to do to help him cross over. "Jimmy, are you still here?" I looked from one side of the cemetery to the other, hoping to catch a glimpse of him or notice some sort of sign that he was okay. But that sign never came. "I understand… This must have taken a lot out of you. Rest, my friend. We'll talk soon." I waved, turned, and sat beside Sara as I closed the car door.

The car ride back to Parker's house was quiet and uneventful, but I wasn't surprised. I was still processing everything that happened, as I'm sure the others were. I was stunned to see it was pushing ten o'clock when Tom dropped us off at Parker's house. Old Man Smithers went directly home after he left. Parker's parents were still in town, so it was just us kids. Another lucky break for me since Sara's mom still hadn't quite forgiven me over the incident at the fire hall dance back in the fall.

Everyone was thrilled with the day's results, and it was easy to understand why. For me, it was a bit different. The thought of not seeing Jimmy when we left the cemetery was disturbing. Had he crossed over? What if his unresolved business was to help Annabelle and Donald cross over to the other side? Where was the other side? Heaven? Or was it down below? I wondered if we would ever know the answers to these questions. Yes, it bothered me. I didn't get to say goodbye. Could he be gone? I thought everyone except for me would all sleep a little easier at night. Jimmy laid heavy on my mind. I needed to talk to him one last time.

Sara stayed close to my side, her breath warm on my neck. We held each other for a long moment. She laid her head on my shoulder. "What are you thinking about?"

"Jimmy." I frowned. "I can't help but wonder how he's doing. Is he alone tonight? Did he cross over? What was his purpose … to help Annabelle and Donald cross over and be together?" Lots of thoughts were racing through my mind.

"What's with the long faces?" Parker interrupted.

"Yeah, we did it. Don't you realize there are no more ghosts?" Buck smiled. "Now we can get on with our lives without all these distractions."

"But what about Jimmy?" The words chirped out of my mouth as a tear rolled down the side of my cheek.

Sara squeezed my hand, and honestly, I hadn't even noticed we were holding hands. Buck, Parker, and Todd looked at one another, then back to me. I saw their hand gestures and watched as they mouthed, "I don't know what to say."

"It's like losing Jimmy all over again," Lexi muttered in a hushed tone.

Scooter pouted. "I never got a chance to say goodbye."

"Me, either." Jimmy beamed as his body manifested before our eyes. The bright light was almost blinding. His smile was contagious as we all jumped at the sight of his pale body before us. I wanted to jump in and give him a big hug, but I knew I would fall flat on my face.

"You gave us all a scare," I mentioned.

"Sorry about that. I was exhausted and needed to vanish to regain some strength."

"Well, don't do that again." Lexi giggled.

We were all excited to see Jimmy. That answered our question about whether he had crossed over. *Now we could say goodbye the way we were meant to.*

"Listen, I'm tired and weak. But I wanted you all to know I'm alright, and thank you for all your help today. I'm grateful." Jimmy flashed us a smile and evaporated as quickly as he arrived.

Fortunately for all of us, Jimmy was still around, but he posed no threat to anyone. He was a good ghost. I couldn't say that about Annabelle or Donald, or even Jacob, although I didn't get to know him that well. We all chatted on the porch for a little longer; then, as the night drew late, I knew it was time to head to the house. Lexi was kind enough to give Buck and me a lift home. I was thankful for that because my eyelids had turned heavy, and I knew I would pass out the minute my head hit the pillow.

Morning came quickly. I slept like a rock and felt better than I had in days. I bounced downstairs and went to the kitchen for a tall glass of milk and a bowl of Quisp cereal. After my shower, I got dressed and told Mother I was heading to the store to help Tom for the day. I knew Tom would be happy to learn Jimmy was still with us, or would he be pleased about that? I wasn't sure at that moment. I guess I'd find out when I told him.

First, I needed to stop by the dam and see if Jimmy was there so we could chat. I grabbed my bike and peddled as fast as possible. In no time, I was pulling into the dam parking lot. I slammed on the brakes, my bike coming to a skidding stop and pebbles flying from underneath my tire, and I laid one of my famous skid marks in the gravel next to the walkway.

I gazed across the long concrete walkway. The dam was empty, with not a person in sight. I pushed my bike down the grass embankment and onto the concrete path. The roar of the water pouring over the dam grew louder as I approached. I stopped and laid my bike down about halfway across the walkway. This spot looked as good as any. "Good morning, Jimmy," I spoke to myself in a normal voice. Not receiving any response from Jimmy, I paused and listened to the pounding sound of the water. It was a beautiful morning. I looked around and watched the water swirl about as it made its way downstream. Light steam rose off the cool water. I wished I had brought my fishing rod with me. I bet the fish would have been biting on a morning like this.

"Jimmy, are you here?" I waited and waited. I felt a little agitated. Why was it that whenever I asked Jimmy to show, he would delay his entrance or not show up? I continued to wait. I looked over my shoulder at the tower. I heard a few birds caw and got excited. A couple of robins were flying around and playing what looked like a game of tag.

I wanted to scream. I was growing tired of waiting. I started to fidget and noticed my foot was thumping on the concrete. Patience was never something I was good at. Ah, who was I kidding? Jimmy wasn't going to show. I felt ridiculous. Why was I waiting for him when he didn't seem to care?

I stood, placing both my hands at the small of my back, and leaned backward, stretching my back the best I could. I listened as my back popped and cracked. *Man, that felt good.* I bounced on the balls of my feet and placed one foot toward my bike. I took another step, followed by another. I guess Jimmy wasn't ready to talk yet. I continued to walk in the direction of my bike until it lay beside my feet. I bent over, grabbed the handlebars, and pulled it upright. I took a deep breath and threw one leg over the upper bar, planting my butt firmly on the seat. I looked over my shoulder one last time before I pushed the pedal downward, and the bike began to roll. Instead of taking Lizardville Road, I decided to take the dirt trail that skirted Big Fishing Creek.

Traveling slowly, I went down a short slope and up the other side of the next hill. I came to the first bend in the creek and coasted my bike to a stop. I watched a few butterflies flitter around and gazed at the water as it rolled past. I took a long look and then started to pedal some more. I went down a long straightaway and slowed my pace at the next turn. The thought of Jimmy burned deep in my mind. Startled by a heart-pounding sound, I stopped and slowly looked around in a circle. I spotted nothing out of the ordinary. Then it dawned on me—I had stopped at our old campsite. I couldn't remember how many times we'd pitched our tents here. I smiled at the memories this place held, dismounted my bike, and sat on one of the old logs around the fire pit. I placed the palms of my hands on my chin and my elbows on my knees and looked out over the water. It was calm and peaceful. I listened to the birds chirp in the distance. The branches of the trees swayed in a light breeze. Bees hummed from plant to plant, and the smell of the forest coming to life filled my nose.

"You okay, Johnny?"

My head snapped upward so quickly that I almost pulled a muscle. I looked around. There was no one there but me. "Who said that?" *Could it have been the wind?*

"Yo, spaz, it's me."

I looked back and forth to no avail. *I guess I am losing my mind.* I'm unsure why that surprised me after everything I'd seen and done.

"Dude, I'm right here," Jimmy whispered in my ear.

I turned my head to the right, and sure enough, Jimmy sat beside me on the log. "I'm so glad to see you." I laughed. "Why didn't you show yourself at the dam?"

"I didn't want anyone to drive past and think you were some crazy kid sitting alone on the dam talking to himself." He grinned.

"Well..." I decided not to finish my sentence. "I'm glad you're here." I paused and swallowed the lump in my throat. "This isn't easy. I want to help. You know that, right?" I frowned.

"Sure do. So, what's on your mind? I mean, you called me out of my sleep."

I knew my question would not be easy to ask. And Jimmy was not making this any easier on me by telling me the answer to the question he knew I wanted to ask. I decided to be straight forward and let the words flow from my mouth. "Can you tell me where your body is located?" The blank expression on my face should have told him how difficult that was for me.

"Sure... when I'm ready," he answered with a smug smile.

I was stunned. I didn't expect Jimmy to pull back and not tell me. I thought that was what he wanted all along. "What do you mean *when you're ready*?"

"What? Are you ready to get rid of me? Dang, that hurts, man," he hissed.

"No, I didn't mean it like that. I'm only trying to help. You know that, right? I thought that's what you wanted?" I pleaded.

"Well, I changed my mind. I don't want to go. I've been thinking about this for some time now. I kind of like being the only ghost around the valley." He snickered.

"What?" I was floored. "What do you mean?"

"What don't you understand, Johnny? I'm staying here. So, don't ask me again where my body is." He shot me a nasty look. "Can you do that?"

Stunned, I nodded and watched as he evaporated before my eyes. I raised a hand to wipe a tear from my cheek. I didn't understand his decision. I sat on that log most of the morning. I thought about how lucky I'd been, how lucky all of us had been. It could have been any one of us that Annabelle possessed that day on the river and forced over the falls. It could have been me who lost my life. But, then again, it was Jimmy who had the puzzle box—the one that Tom gave him. If anyone was to blame, maybe it was Tom. I'm not sure why I was trying to blame someone, maybe out of guilt because I survived. If anyone was to blame, it was Annabelle—she was the one who took Jimmy's life.

I wondered what happened to Annabelle and Donald Thornhill. Were they together? Did the two of them really cross over? And if they did, were they sent to Heaven, or were they sent to shovel coal? And Jacob, was he at peace? I guess I'll never know the answers to those questions. I'm not even sure Jimmy knows the answers to those questions.

The boys looked on, waiting for me to finish. I frowned and thought about my life. What if Annabelle had chosen me instead of Jimmy? I would have never married or had any kids. I would have stayed the same age as Jimmy. The memories still haunt me today. I wiped another tear off my cheek.

"So, what happened after that?" Zack asked.

"Did you ever see Jimmy again? Did you cross him over? Don't leave us hanging, Dad," Daniel pleaded.

"Well, there's not much more I can say. No, I never saw or spoke to Jimmy again. There were times when I knew he was watching me. Sara said she felt his presence from time to time too. As did Scooter, Todd, Buck, Parker, and Lexi. It's a feeling that's hard to describe. We knew he was there, watching, observing, but he never showed himself."

I'm unsure if Jimmy felt like an outcast or even a loner as he watched the rest of us grow older. He would never age; he'd always be that thirteen-year-old Wildman we knew as a kid. Tom Evans continued running the store, and I worked there until graduation. Old Man Smithers went back to hating us kids—I guess he wanted to forget about that day in the cemetery.

Eventually, we all grew up, dated, worked, drove cars, and graduated high school. Some of us went to college, others joined the military, and some, like Parker, went straight into the workforce. The one thing we all did was move away from Lizardville. I'm not sure if Jimmy resented us for getting older or leaving him behind. I wish we could have talked one last time, at least gotten the chance to explain, but that never happened.

"What about the puzzle box? What happened to it, and who had it?" Daniel asked.

"Well, I never saw the thing after that day in the cave. Now I'll be thinking about that for the next few weeks. I might even ask Sara to see if she remembers. I'm unsure if Old Man Smithers kept the box like Jimmy had said or if he buried it with Jacob in the cemetery."

"The next time we go back to visit family, will you take us to the factory and dam?" Daniel asked. "I want to meet Jimmy." For a second, I thought he was concerned for Jimmy.

"That would be awesome," Zack added. "I'll get some pictures and post them on social media," Zack smiled.

"Yes, we'll be famous, the brothers who saw a ghost," Daniel added.

"Stop." I gave them both a stern look. "Jimmy was my friend, and he has feelings," I frowned and paused. The boys bowed and gave me their sad faces. I was always a sucker for that. "Maybe, just maybe, I'll take you to visit the factory and dam when you are older, much older. But you might be disappointed to learn Jimmy hasn't appeared in years."

The boys could tell I was troubled by how things ended with Jimmy, but they only stared at me. The hum of the refrigerator coming to life caught our attention, as did the lights flashing throughout the house. The power had been restored, and the storm was nearing its end. I watched the boys bounce from their chairs and head to their bedrooms. "Thanks for the story, Dad," Daniel called back.

"Yeah, thanks, Dad," Zack bellowed from the hallway.

A great feeling rushed over me. *I'm glad the boys had the opportunity to hear about my childhood experiences. Lizardville was a great place to grow up. Now my memories will live on forever. But how will Sara feel about my promise to take the boys to the axe factory and dam?* Well, I'll deal with that later.

My phone buzzed. Relief flooded me as I read a text from Sara. She was on her way home.

# ACKNOWLEDGMENTS

W riting is a lonely job. I spend many hours a day cooped up in my office with no one to talk with. But I'm grateful for the time to do what I love and enjoy. Thank you to my loving wife, Toni, for all your patience, support, ideas, and help while I was writing this story.

Thank you to my four wonderful daughters, Kim, Kelly, Jessica, and Ashley, for all your encouragement.

Thank you to my parents, Charlie and Joanne, for believing in me and buying a home on Lizardville Road.

Special thanks to my Editor, Gayle Staggemeyer, for your sharp eye and helpful hints. I couldn't have done this without you. You took my manuscript and added your magical touch to help make this story what it is today.

Thank you, Phoenix Whirl, Teresa Allaert Thompson, Silvia Curry, and Melissa Derr, for your thoughts and suggestions while proofreading the story.

Learn more about Steve Altier and his stories by following him on social media or visiting his website www.stevealtier.com. Steve would love to hear from you. You can drop him a line at stevealtierbooks@outlook.com.

# BOOK CLUB QUESTIONS

1. What did you think of the writing? Are there any standout sentences?

2. Would you want to read another book by this author?

3. Did you guess the ending? If so, at what point?

4. Which twist surprised you the most?

5. If you could ask the author anything, what would it be?

6. How does the book's title work in relation to the book's contents? If you could give the book a new title, what would it be?

7. Would you ever consider re-reading it? Why or why not?

8.  Are there lingering questions from the book you're still thinking about?

9.  Did the book frighten you or get under your skin in any way?

10. Which characters did you like best? Which did you like least?

11. If you had to trade places with one character, who would it be?

12. What did you think of the book's length? If it's too long, what would you cut? If too short, what would you add?

13. What songs does this book make you think of? Create a book group playlist together!

14. Which character in the book would you most like to meet?

15. Which places in the book would you most like to visit?

16. Did the book strike you as original?

17. What do you think of the book's cover? How well does it convey what the book is about? If the book has been published with different covers, which one do you like best?

18. What other books by this author have you read? How did they compare to this book?

19. Was the pacing—beginning, middle, and end—
    done well?

20. If you could hear this same story from another person's
    point of view, who would you choose?

# AUTHOR BIO

**S**teve Altier is a bestselling paranormal, mystery, and suspense writer. He is known for his multi-award-winning series, *The Lizardville Ghost Stories*, and Amazon Bestseller, *The Ghost Hunter*. Steve grew up in a small town in central Pennsylvania. His parents owned the dam keeper's house on Lizardville Road. Across the street was an old, broken-down dam and the remnants of the ax factory. Steve and his buddies spent many days exploring the abandoned factory. Unexplained things happened when Steve was a child—inspiring his love for everything spooky, along with many of his stories. Steve currently lives in Florida with his wife, four daughters, and four cats.